GABRIEL

SHADOWRIDGE GUARDIANS MC

BECCA JAMESON

COVER MODEL
JOSE BARREIRO

ABOUT SHADOWRIDGE GUARDIANS MC

Combining the sizzling talents of bestselling authors **Pepper North, Kate Oliver, and Becca Jameson, the Shadowridge Guardians are guaranteed to give you a thrill and leave you dreaming of your own throbbing motorcycle joyride.**

Are you daring enough to ride with a club of rough, growly, commanding men? The protective Daddies of the Shadowridge Guardians Motorcycle Club will stop at nothing to ensure the safety and protection of everything that belongs to them: their Littles, their club, and their town. Throw in some sassy, naughty, mischievous women who won't hesitate to serve their fair share of attitude even in the face of looming danger, and this brand new MC Romance series is ready to ignite!

Shadowridge Guardians MC
Steele by Pepper North
Kade by Kate Oliver
Atlas by Becca Jameson
Doc by Kate Oliver
Gabriel by Becca Jameson

Talon by Pepper North
Bear by Becca Jameson
Faust by Pepper North
Storm by Kate Oliver

Gabriel

"Ladybug, you're about to become intimately acquainted with my palm..."

Eden's life is falling apart. In response to sexual harassment from unruly customers and her boss, she has quit her job and walked out of the diner. Alone on the street, scared out of her mind, and frantic, she accepts help from one of the members of the Shadowridge Guardians.

Gabriel is known among MC members as the wise one. He knows everything about every member, and takes his job as advisor seriously. His life is tidy and in control...until he heads to the town diner to pick up the tear-streaked, high-energy, fast-talking Little girl in desperate need of a Daddy.

Eden brings Gabriel to his knees in a heartbeat, but what she really needs is to be taken *over* his knees.

CHAPTER
ONE

"Carlee?" Eden could barely get her friend's name out between sobs as she held her cell phone close to her ear.

"Eden? What's wrong? Where are you?" Carlee asked.

Eden stopped walking and looked around, sniffling. "I need help," she admitted reluctantly. "I'm scared." She couldn't stop shaking.

There was a shuffling sound, and then Carlee's boyfriend was on the phone. "Eden, honey, where are you?" Atlas asked.

Tears streamed down her cheeks. "About a block from the diner, I think." A sob escaped. "I ran out. I think I went left. I wasn't thinking."

"Okay, honey, I'm sending someone to help you. His name is Gabriel Marcos. Stay right where you are and keep talking to me," he ordered.

Eden had met Atlas several times. She knew he was a good guy and treated Carlee like spun gold. She also knew he was a member of the Shadowridge Guardians MC.

Before Carlee had started dating Atlas, Eden had always been a bit nervous when members of the Shadowridge

Guardians came into the diner. She'd since realized they were some of the best guys on the planet.

"Eden?" Atlas prodded. "Are you with me, honey?"

"Y-yes, Sir."

"Good girl. Keep talking to me."

"Is G-Gabriel one of your, uh, brothers?" *Is that what they call each other?*

"He sure is, honey. He's a super good guy. I promise."

"O-okay." She sniffled again as she hugged herself. She was still wearing her apron. She hadn't even stopped to grab her purse before she'd run out of the diner.

"I can hear the motorcycle engine through the phone, honey. He's almost there."

Eden realized he was right. She was glad he was still talking to her. The approaching motorcycle might have scared her otherwise. Sure enough, it was coming into view from her left.

"H-he's here," she muttered as the motorcycle pulled to a stop.

"Okay, honey. Let Gabriel help you."

The man who parked alongside her kicked out the stand, rose from the bike, and pulled his helmet off in seconds. He rushed over to her. "Eden?"

She wanted to stop crying, but she couldn't. More tears fell. She was trembling so badly she almost dropped her phone.

The tall man gently took the cell from her and spoke into it. "I've got her, Atlas." He ended the call and pocketed the phone before squatting in front of her. "You're safe, Eden. Can you tell me what happened?"

Suddenly, she felt stupid. Maybe she'd overreacted. She started crying harder now. "I-I d-didn't know w-what to d-do. I'm sorry." She swiped at the tears, trying to banish them, but more kept coming.

"You did the right thing, Little one. You called for help."

"I'm s-sorry to be a b-bother."

"No reason to be sorry." He rose to his full height, turned around, and opened the saddlebag on his bike. A moment later, he held out a cute, fluffy, brown teddy bear. "How about you hold this little fellow for me? I bet he'll make you feel better."

She took him and pulled him against her chest. He was adorable. "W-whose b-bear is this?"

"Yours, Little one. I bet he's super happy to finally get out of my bag and into the hands of a Little girl."

"I'm n-not l-little. I'm twenty-six, Sir." She suspected that when he called her little he wasn't referring to size or age. After all, she was aware that Carlee's relationship with Atlas was a special kind of arrangement in which she called Atlas her Daddy, and he took care of her like a Little girl.

Before meeting Atlas, Eden hadn't known such relationships existed, but from the moment she'd seen the two of them together, she'd felt jealous. She'd also started reading books and researching age play. She'd told herself it was so she could better understand her friend, that she'd been intrigued, but the truth was she'd learned more about herself than anything else.

Gabriel smiled at her as he ran his fingers through his thick hair to pull it back from his face. The dark hair was several inches long and curly. In contrast, his beard was gray—almost white. "Little girls come in all ages and sizes, Eden," he informed her.

She nodded slowly, sniffling.

"Let's get you someplace comfortable and safe, okay?" He turned toward the saddlebag again and pulled out a helmet. This one was pink and smaller than his. It was made for a woman. Like the teddy bear, she wondered who usually wore the helmet.

"I've n-never b-been on a b-bike," she admitted as he pulled the helmet over her head.

He fastened it under her chin and tipped her head back.

His smile was warm and inviting. "Then you're in for a treat." He climbed onto the bike and held out a hand.

She stared at him. "I d-don't know about t-this," she whimpered, feeling silly.

"Put your foot on the peg here and swing your leg over."

She shuffled slowly forward, her heart racing now for a new reason. The fear she'd been feeling before he arrived was being replaced by a new fear. Maybe that was a good thing.

"Nothing will happen to you, Little one. I promise."

She finally grabbed his arm, set her foot on the peg, and swung her leg over. "Oh," she exclaimed as her entire body came into contact with his.

He popped his own helmet back on and started up the engine. "Wrap your arms tightly around me, Eden. The teddy bear will be protected between us."

Maybe this was a bad idea. Maybe she should have found her wits and headed for the bus stop like she normally would. The problem was she'd been so panicked when she'd run out of the diner that she hadn't even gone in the right direction, and she'd been afraid to double back.

"Hold on tight."

She wasn't about to let go, and even though she was scared, she felt exhilarated as he took off. The wind hit her cheeks and dried her tears. It felt good against her heated skin.

Holding on to this gorgeous man was no hardship either. She shuddered as she pressed closer to him. The position was so erotic, with her legs spread wide against his thighs and her chest pressed against his back.

She closed her eyes, took deep breaths, and felt her body relax as they got farther from the diner. She couldn't imagine what she was going to do next with her life. However, for at least a few minutes, she would absorb the strength of her savior and let him protect her.

When he slowed down and leaned them to the right to turn, she opened her eyes. Her breath hitched. He hadn't taken her home. He'd brought her to the motorcycle club. *Duh. You didn't give him your address, dork.*

She didn't say a word because the truth was she would feel safer inside the compound than alone at her apartment. Maybe he'd brought her here to be with Carlee. That made sense.

Gabriel parked, shut off the engine, and removed his helmet before twisting his neck around to look at her. He wore that grin again. "As much as I love the feel of your arms around me, Little one, you're going to have to let go if you want to go inside."

She gasped and immediately released her tight grip, embarrassed.

He eased himself off the bike before reaching for her hips, lifting her off, and setting her feet on the ground. After unfastening the chin strap, he pulled the helmet very carefully off her head. "I don't want to pull your pretty curls, Eden."

She groaned. "Maybe if you pull them hard enough, they'll get straighter and won't be so annoying."

He frowned as he lifted a lock. "I would never pull them hard enough to hurt, Little one, unless, of course, you asked me to." He chuckled. "I love these wild red curls." He leaned in closer and whispered in her ear conspiratorially, "I have a soft spot for Little girls with red curly hair and green eyes. I think it's my lucky day."

Her breath hitched. "You're just saying that to make me feel better."

He took her shoulders and met her gaze. "I may say a lot of things to help you feel better because I can't stand to see a Little girl sad, but I will never lie. I love your hair, Little one." He twirled a curl around one finger.

She stared at him wide-eyed. The way he kept calling her Little one made her heart race. Even though she'd been exploring the aspects of age play, she'd never acted on any of her bourgeoning feelings, and she certainly hadn't met a Daddy other than Atlas.

"Come." He nodded over his shoulder and took her hand.

"Where are we going?" she asked. She was no longer crying, but the threat of doing so again as soon as she let herself think about what had happened made her swallow back a knot in her throat.

"To my suite, Little one."

"Your suite?" Her voice squeaked. She didn't know this man. Not really. What if he expected her to sleep with him or something since he'd been kind enough to pick her up?

Then she remembered that Carlee and Atlas had sent him to get her. Carlee would never send a bad man to help her. Neither would Atlas.

She had to kind of skip to keep up with him, but when he glanced back, he slowed. "I'm sorry. I haven't taken care of a Little girl for a long time. I forget I need to slow my pace."

As they stepped inside the main building of the compound, Eden held her breath. She hadn't been here before. She had no idea what to expect. It was a motorcycle club, so she assumed there would be half-naked women, drunken men pawing at them, and probably drugs.

When they entered the main room, she was surprised to see only a few people in the giant living space. A woman wearing all black was curled up on the couch with her head on a man's lap. She was watching cartoons and had a two-handled sippy cup in her grip.

The man was stroking her hair. He nodded toward Gabriel but didn't say a word. Two other men were sitting at a table across the room playing chess. They also gave Gabriel a polite nod.

Everything she'd ever thought about motorcycle clubs went out the window. No one was having sex. It was quiet. There was no debauchery at all.

Gabriel led her toward a hallway, where he finally stopped, unlocked a door, and opened it. He held it wide for her. "Ladies first."

She ducked under his arm to enter. Once again, she was stunned. This was an ordinary apartment. There was a small living room, an attached kitchenette, and three doors leading to other rooms.

Gabriel shut and locked the door before turning to her.

She gasped when his hands came to her waist, thinking he was about to pull her shirt off or something, but when she looked down, she found him untying her apron. She'd run out of the diner so fast she was still wearing it.

He untied it, pulled it over her head, and tossed it aside before pointing toward the couch. "Sit, Little one. I'll get you a drink. Would you like juice, milk, or water?"

"Umm. Do you have apple juice?" she asked tentatively. She hadn't had apple juice in a long time. It sounded good. She lowered onto the couch and set the bear at her side, feeling kind of silly holding it.

"Of course. What kind of Daddy would I be if I didn't have an emergency stash of apple juice?"

Daddy... So, he was definitely a Daddy. Like Atlas. The thought made her lick her lips. He was being so kind to her. She'd never even had a boyfriend treat her as well as this stranger had in the last half an hour.

When he returned and held out a cup, she stared at it for a moment before taking it from him. "Thank you," she whispered. It was a sippy cup like the one she'd seen the woman in the living room holding. It had two handles and a spill-proof spout to drink from.

He sat next to her, his body turned slightly toward her, and tucked a curl behind her ear. She figured her hair was wild and unruly, but he seemed to stare as if she were the most beautiful creature on earth.

"Take a drink, Eden. You'll feel better. Then you can tell me what happened."

She lifted the sippy cup and tipped it back, almost missing her lips.

"Use both hands, Little one," he encouraged.

She lifted her other hand to steady the cup and center it. It was easier that way, but she felt strange drinking from it. She felt even stranger obeying him. Butterflies fluttered in her tummy.

Despite all the reading and studying she'd done about age play lately, she'd never actually practiced the kink, nor had she ever met another Daddy besides Atlas. She felt oddly comfortable.

"Good girl," he praised, his fingers stroking the edge of her jaw.

Those two words did something to her. She felt decidedly Littler. *Am I Little?* Just because she liked the way it made her feel to read about it didn't mean she would like to actually practice it.

"Feel better?"

"Yes, Sir," she murmured. For some reason, it felt right and natural to address him as Sir.

He seemed pleased because he smiled. "Good. Now, tell me what happened. Atlas said you were working at the diner tonight?"

"Uh-huh." She nodded and then looked down at her lap. She was wearing her nicest jeans and a white T-shirt. Nothing special. Marv didn't require the waitresses to wear a uniform as long as they wore his apron when they were on shift.

When she thought about telling Gabriel what had happened, she groaned inside. She didn't want to talk about it. She pursed her lips.

"Tell me," he encouraged as he took the sippy cup and set it on the coffee table. "Did someone hurt you?"

She shuddered. "Not really..." she murmured. Her face heated.

"I promise you'll feel better if you let it all out."

"It was nothing really."

"I don't believe that. Little girls don't run out of work crying and calling for help after nothing happens."

She glanced up at him. "I'm being stupid. Maybe it was my fault."

His brows lifted. "Do not use that word again, Eden. I won't have you calling yourself names. Understood?"

Her cheeks heated further. "Yes, Sir," she whispered.

"How about you let me decide."

She licked her lips and drew in a breath. Apparently, he wasn't going to stop hounding her until she told him. "There were these four men at the diner having dinner. I hate it when they come in. They make me nervous."

He frowned. "Do you know who they are?"

"No, but they wear leather vests and stuff like you, but the logo isn't a teddy bear. It's like a red jester."

Gabriel's jaw tightened. "The Devil's Jesters. They're a gang from another town. They aren't good people."

She rubbed her hands on her thighs.

"What happened, Little one?" he encouraged.

"They were making crude comments every time I brought something to their table, making fun of my body and stuff. They even asked if my hair matched my..." She trailed off, not wanting to say that out loud.

Gabriel's entire body stiffened. He growled, too. After slowly closing and reopening his eyes, he said, "Go on." His voice was calm for her but held an edge of fury.

"I can ignore their words. Sticks and stones and all that. I don't like it when people talk to me like that, but they're just words."

"But..."

She drew in another slow breath. "I was bringing one of them a fresh soda, but when I bent to set it on the table, the man closest to the edge of the booth reached out and pinched my butt."

"He fucking touched you?" Gabriel blurted.

"I should've just ignored him and walked away." She started shaking again. "I overreacted."

"What did you do, Little one?"

"I hadn't set the glass down yet, so I turned and tossed the soda in his face."

Gabriel smiled. "Good girl."

Her eyes widened. "I don't think that was my best course of action. He jumped up and started screaming at me. He called me names I've never even heard before. Every customer in the diner was staring at us. Then Marv came out from the back room. He was furious and started lecturing me in front of everyone about how to treat the customers. When I told him that man had touched me, he said to grow up, and he called me worse names than the Jester guy. So, I ran out of the diner." She dropped her face.

Tears started falling again as she realized the implications of her actions. "There's no way he'll take me back," she sobbed, putting her palms over her face. "I'll never be able to pay my rent. I needed that job."

Gabriel surprised her by tucking a hand under her knees, setting the other at her back, and lifting her off the couch to settle her on his lap. He rubbed her back as he pressed her cheek against his shoulder. "You did the right thing. No one has the right to yell at another person, but they most definitely don't have the right to touch them. Your boss, Marv, is an asshole. You're not going back there, Little girl."

She cried harder. "I-I n-needed that j-job."

"No one needs that kind of job, nor do they deserve to be abused, Eden." He rocked her back and forth for a long time. "Let it all out, Little girl. I've got you."

When she finally stopped sobbing and only the occasional sniffle remained, she wiped her eyes.

Gabriel leaned to one side, snagged a tissue from a box on the end table, and handed it to her. "Blow your nose, Little one."

She did as he suggested. "I'm sorry. I'm such a baby. I over-reacted."

"Look at me, Eden," he commanded.

She lifted her gaze.

"You did not overreact. You did exactly the right thing. You got out of an abusive situation and called for help." He reached across her, picked up the stuffed bear, and handed it to her. "I bet if you hold this little guy, you'll feel better. Stuffies always make Little girls feel better."

"How do you know I'm Little?" she asked, meeting his gaze.

He smiled. "Daddies just know these things. I have Little-girl radar," he teased.

"I've never had a Daddy. I've never even met one, except Atlas, of course."

"Well, now you have, and I'm so glad you never met one before me."

Her brow furrowed. "Why?"

"Because he might have snatched you up and made you his. I'm relieved to know you don't already have a Daddy because that means I can be your Daddy."

Eden gasped. *He can be my Daddy?*

CHAPTER
TWO

G abriel was both furious and elated. He hated that Eden had been treated so badly, but he was beyond grateful that Atlas had called him and sent him to get her. He'd known almost from the moment he'd stepped off his bike that he would soon be fully wrapped around her sweet finger.

She stared at him wide-eyed. "You don't even know me."

"I know everything I need to know to feel the connection deep in my heart. Can you feel it, too, Little one?" He set a hand on her chest.

She didn't respond. That seemed promising.

"Now, here's what we're going to do. You'll stay here tonight. Tomorrow, I'll go talk to Marv and find out who specifically was in the diner last night, and—"

She gasped and shook her head. "He'll be furious." And then she groaned. "Oh, shit. I left my purse there. My ID is in it."

He lifted a hand and tapped her lips. "Don't cuss, Little girl. Daddy's rules."

Did she shudder? He was pretty confident she did. And her cheeks pinkened further. "Yes, Sir," she whispered.

God, he loved it when she called him Sir, but he'd love it even more when she started calling him Daddy. Soon. "Don't you worry about Marv. I don't care if he's furious. He's all bluff and hot air. The man probably hasn't worked out a day in his life. I could take him on blindfolded with one arm tied behind my back and knock him out in ten seconds."

She gasped. "You can't hit him. You might get arrested."

He smiled. "I won't have to hit him. I promise. I'm pretty convincing with just my words. I'll get your purse back, find out who touched you, and make it clear you will not be returning."

"But I need that job," she wailed.

"Little girl, no one needs that job."

Her voice rose. "I won't be able to pay my bills," she repeated.

"Then you'll stay here. I'll help you get back on your feet, Little one."

"I can't ask you to do that."

"You didn't. I offered."

"Maybe you should take me home," she murmured. "I don't want to be any trouble."

"You're not trouble, and never refer to yourself as such again. I wouldn't take you home even if I didn't believe in my heart that you're mine, Eden. It's not safe. Those men aren't good men. If they're angry enough—and I'm betting they are —they probably went straight to your apartment to watch for you to arrive. I bet they're there now."

She gasped. "How would they know where I live?"

"I'm sure Marv was happy to give them your personal information if they asked for it. Marv is an ass-kisser. All he cares about is making money. He wouldn't want the Devil's Jesters to stop coming into his diner."

She shuddered and looked away. Her next words changed the air in the room and made him chuckle. "How come you get to cuss, and I don't?"

"Because I'm the Daddy, and you're the Little girl. I make the rules. You break the rules. That's how it works."

She swallowed. "What happens if I break the rules?"

"Then I discipline you," he informed her, watching her closely. She was friends with Carlee, so he had to assume she wasn't totally ignorant about age play. She might not have practiced it before, but she'd apparently done some research and knew in her heart she might be Little.

She was hugging that bear close to her chest. Did she know she was petting its fur and sometimes rubbed her chin or nose against the soft fluff? "Discipline me how?" she asked softly.

"Depends on what works for you, Little one. Usually, I'd take you over my knee and spank your naughty bottom."

She squirmed deliciously on his lap, but the most telling sign was the way she squeezed her thighs together, and damn if she didn't hug the bear even tighter. He'd bet money she was pressing him against her hard nipples.

"You would spank me?" she asked, her voice pitching higher.

"I *will* definitely spank you, Little girl. Often, I presume. Sometimes, I will do so to discipline you. Other times, I will do so to give you the release you crave from stress. I bet you'd feel a whole lot better right now if I spanked you," he pointed out, watching her closely.

Those eyes were so pretty. The green was mesmerizing. Every time she widened them, his cock stiffened. "I don't think I would like to be spanked, Sir," she whispered.

"Mmm. Don't knock it until you've tried it. Most Little girls find it cathartic. They misbehave on purpose just to get their naughty bottoms spanked."

She gasped. He loved it when she gasped in shock. He loved that she was rather green about age play, and he would be the one to teach her and guide her.

"What's your full name, Eden?"

"Eden Jane Zimbel."

"Eden Jane Zimbel... Now, I'll know what to yell out when you're in trouble." He winked at her.

Her eyes widened.

He chuckled and slid his hand up to her neck, using a firm, exaggerated voice to try out a full reprimand. "Eden Jane Zimbel... What did I say about running in the clubhouse?"

She giggled. "That's silly."

He pulled her closer. "I like the way it sounds."

She looked around the room. "Do you have a guest room?"

He shook his head. "No, but you can take my bed. I'll sleep out here on the couch."

"I don't even have jammies," she argued adorably.

"You can wear one of my shirts, Little one. It will hang to your knees." He lifted her off his lap reluctantly and set her on her feet. It was late. He needed to let her shower and get some sleep. "How about a shower or a bath?"

"Okay," she murmured. "I'm pretty sticky from the diner. I think some of the soda splashed in my hair, too."

"Then let's get you cleaned up and tucked in." He rose and took her hand to lead her into his bedroom and through to the bathroom.

"Do you live here?"

"Yep. It's not much, but it's all I need. The other room is my office. I work from home. I need to be available at the compound as often as possible because I'm also the club's chaplain."

"Oh."

"The kitchen is small," he continued as he pulled out a clean towel and washcloth, "but I eat most of my meals in the main dining room with the rest of the club members." He turned toward her. "Atlas and Carlee have a suite like mine but don't usually spend the night. They could, though, anytime."

"Oh," she said again.

"Now, here's a towel," he patted it, "and there's soap,

shampoo, and conditioner on the rack in the shower. If you'd rather take a bath, I can move them into the tub."

She shook her head. "A shower is fine. Thank you. I really appreciate you helping me. I promise I'll go home tomorrow to figure things out and get out of your hair."

He cupped her face and tipped her head back to make sure he had her full attention. "Eden, I won't pressure you to return my feelings, but I'm serious about being your Daddy. I can feel it in my bones. You won't be getting out of my hair ever, nor will I drop you off at home and leave you vulnerable to the Devil's Jesters. From now on, you're my responsibility. I will take care of you and make sure you're safe. I will deal with the men who touched and made fun of you so it won't happen again." He leaned in closer. "This is your home now, too, Little one."

Her pretty eyes couldn't have gone wider if she'd tried. "But…"

He shook his head. "No buts. Let me grab you a T-shirt so you can put it on after your shower. Put the rest of your clothes in the hamper, Little one. Okay?"

She glanced at it. "Okay."

"Good girl." He hated releasing her to leave her standing there alone while he hurried to his dresser to grab a T-shirt. He also hated leaving her alone in the bathroom. He would much rather take her clothes off himself, lower her into the tub, and bathe her like he intended to do for the rest of their lives.

But Eden wasn't ready for him to be quite that high-handed with her tonight. She'd had a terrible fright. She was shaking and scared. Getting naked in front of him would be more than she could handle.

One night, though. Tomorrow night, he intended to get past this stage. He wouldn't have sex with her until she was fully ready to commit to him, but he most certainly would take care of her in every way tomorrow, and the day would end with a bath and his hands all over her sweet body.

"Need anything else, Little one?" he asked as he returned to set the shirt on top of the towel. He also found a new toothbrush in one of the drawers.

She shook her head. "No, Sir."

He smiled at her. "I can't wait until you're comfortable enough to call me Daddy." He stepped toward the door. "I'll leave this door ajar in case you need me. Just call out. I'll be close by."

She looked dazed but didn't say anything as he stepped out of the room, leaving the door open about two inches. He barely had the strength to leave her to bathe alone. No way could he also shut the door, completely separating them.

As he paced the room, he listened to her shuffling around. The water came on. The shower door opened and closed. The thought of her naked and so close to him made his cock protest.

He needed to distract himself, and he did so by reminding himself what he would be facing tomorrow. His first stop would be the diner. It opened pretty fucking early. He would be there damn early, too. He would get her purse and have some words with Marv.

That man was a world-class asshole. He'd treated Carlee like scum when she'd worked there. Apparently, the shitbag treated all the waitresses the same way. What a chauvinist pig.

Gabriel would get the names of the four Devil's Jesters out of Marv and then meet with his brothers to figure out what to do. One thing was for sure—Eden wouldn't be safe until something was done. The Jesters weren't the type of men to take kindly to being made to look foolish, and Gabriel's Little girl had definitely done exactly that.

Gabriel paced while Eden took her shower. His life had taken a one-eighty so fast his head was spinning. He'd spent years without a Little girl, but only because he hadn't ever met the right one. It was funny how he'd known Eden was his so fast. He felt emotionally knocked on his ass.

He was also elated. Thank goodness he didn't have anything pressing happening with work this week because he suspected he would need to devote the majority of his time to helping his Little girl acclimate.

Eden would need gentle guidance as she learned what it meant to be his Little girl. He suspected she was also going to challenge him every step of the way. He'd seen how she'd fidgeted when he'd suggested spanking her. The Little stinker was going to enjoy it.

He turned toward his bed. He'd washed the sheets just that morning. He wondered if she normally slept with a stuffie. The bear was the only one he had in his room, but he could get one from the supply closet if she needed it to sleep. Maybe he should do that...? But he didn't want to leave her. So, no.

When the water turned off, he took several deep breaths. Show time.

CHAPTER
THREE

Eden tried not to think about what would happen when she left the bathroom. It was strange having the door open, even slightly. She kept worrying he might see her through the crack, though she wasn't sure why she cared. So what if he saw her?

After drying off, she quickly hung up the towel and pulled his T-shirt over her head. At least she was covered now. She wasn't ready for him to see her pale skin or the scattering of freckles. She'd never been fond of her coloring, but she was stuck with it.

She groaned inside her head as she worked a comb through her curls. She needed a haircut. Her red curls were tight enough that they got unruly when they were too long.

Gabriel seemed to like them, though. He'd insisted he would not lie to her.

Shaking off her wandering thoughts, she brushed her teeth and then turned to face the door. She couldn't stay in here forever. She needed to face the sexy man who insisted he was her Daddy, even though she barely understood what that might entail.

Inching the door open, she finally got brave enough to step

into the room, where she found him sitting on the edge of the bed.

"Did you brush your teeth, Little one?"

"Yes, Sir."

"How about your clothes? Did you put them in the hamper?"

She turned around to see them lying on the floor where she'd taken them off. She'd put them in a tidy pile so he wouldn't see her panties or bra, but apparently, he'd been serious about the hamper, so she turned back around, scooped up her clothes, and put them into the basket on top of his clothes.

It felt so intimate, and though she had no real idea what it felt like to be Little, she was catching on. Obeying his orders made her feel very Little.

"Good girl." He patted the bed beside him where he'd turned down the blankets. "Come. You have to be exhausted."

She shuffled toward him. All she was wearing was his T-shirt. She'd considered putting her panties back on, but she hadn't wanted to pull dirty panties over her clean body. Maybe she should have.

As she got closer, she realized she had a new problem. His bed was very high. She was only five-four. She wouldn't be able to climb up gracefully, and she certainly wouldn't be able to do so without him seeing her private parts.

He rose as she approached, lifted her by the hips, and settled her onto the bed.

She gasped as she tugged the T-shirt down over her bottom and made sure it covered her completely.

He chuckled. "You won't have secrets from Daddy, Little one. I know you're tired and still shook up from what happened this evening, so I didn't want to add to your stress by undressing you and bathing you tonight, but you should know I intend to take care of all your needs, starting tomorrow." He lifted a brow as he pulled the covers over her and sat on the edge of the bed.

She squirmed at the thought of this man taking over her life. It was happening so fast. Her head was spinning. She wasn't altogether opposed to the idea either, which made her even more nervous.

She really needed to talk to Carlee. "Where's Carlee?" she asked in a soft voice.

"She and Atlas are out of town. They went away for the weekend. I'll call Atlas as soon as I get you settled and let him know you're okay. I'm sure Carlee will be anxious to see you when they get back in a few days."

The thought of not getting to see Carlee so she could sort out her feelings with someone who would understand made her tense. Tears welled up in the corners of her eyes again. She couldn't stop them.

"Hey, there. Why the new tears?" He lifted a hand and wiped them away with his thumb.

"I don't have many close friends," she murmured, feeling foolish. "And-and I'm confused. I need to talk to Carlee." Her lip trembled. It wouldn't matter if she had ten thousand close friends; there was no way she would discuss what she was feeling tonight with anyone but Carlee. Carlee was the only friend she knew who practiced some form of age play.

Gabriel set a hand on the top of her head. "Take a deep breath. No need to panic. I know I've thrown a lot at you in a short amount of time. I'm sure Atlas already has Carlee tucked in for the night, but I'll check and see if she can talk to you tomorrow morning, okay?"

Eden nodded. If she tried to talk, she would cry. She was so emotional. She was also stunned that Gabriel wasn't judging her. He didn't seem the least bit put out by her waterworks.

"Now," he said with a twinkle in his eye, "I have an important question."

She pursed her lips, nervous to hear what he might ask.

"Do you have a special friend you usually sleep with at night?"

She sucked in a breath and held it. She couldn't tell him that.

"No reason to be embarrassed, Little one. Most Little girls have special stuffies. Some have dozens of them. I'm sure there's a variety in the supply closet in the hallway if you like a certain type, or you can snuggle with Mr. Bear tonight." He lifted the stuffed bear from the pillow next to her and held it up.

Eden cautiously reached out to take the bear before pulling him under the covers. He wasn't Spot, but he would do for tonight. "His name can't be Mr. Bear," she informed him without thinking.

"Oh? What should he be named?"

She shrugged, thinking. "Coco, I think."

He smiled. "Why Coco?"

"Because he's the color of chocolate, and I love chocolate." How did Gabriel make it so easy to be with him?

"Coco, it is. Will he do for the night until we can get your things from your apartment tomorrow?"

"How do you know I have stuffed animals at my apartment?" she asked skeptically.

"It's not too much of a stretch. For one thing, even though you might not have outwardly realized you were Little, I suspect you have tendencies that would've tipped me off no matter how or when I'd met you. I bet you have some toys you enjoy playing with." He lifted his brow again.

Her face heated. "I don't play with toys. I'm too old to play with toys."

He gasped as if she'd said something horrifying.

Eden giggled, feeling lighter than she had all evening. Gabriel did that to her.

"No one is too old to play with toys, especially not pretty

Little girls with adorable red curls and tiny freckles on their noses," he teased as he tapped her nose.

"Red hair and freckles are not pretty," she reminded him.

Both brows went up. "I believe I mentioned having a soft spot in my heart for red curls on Little girls."

"Yeah, but..." She wasn't sure how to continue. He would be mad if she accused him of lying.

"Do you need me to flip you over and spank your naughty bottom until you believe me, Eden?"

She shook her head rapidly as she squeezed her thighs together. "No, Sir."

"Mmm." He seemed to contemplate the idea. He even tapped his lips. "Okay, this is your last pass, though. Not one more negative word about your pretty hair or any other part of your body."

She turned her head away. It was hard to believe he wasn't just saying that to be nice. She'd spent her entire life being made fun of.

His hand came to her cheek. "Hey there," he said gently. "Tell me what you're thinking."

"People don't like red hair," she admitted without looking at him.

He gasped. "What people?"

She shrugged. "Most people."

"I don't know any of these people, and I'm certainly not one of them. I think you're the prettiest Little girl I've ever seen." He leaned closer and added, "You're also a beautiful woman, Eden. Did someone tell you otherwise?"

Her lip trembled. "Adults are too polite to say mean things, but kids aren't, and I was a kid once."

"Oh, sweet girl. I'm so sorry. Did kids say mean things to you at school?"

She nodded and pursed her lips.

"Well, they were mean bullies. I bet half of them were jealous."

She released her lips and gasped, looking at him.

He nodded. "That's right. Most of them had boring, straight brown hair. They were jealous that you had pretty red curls. Jealousy makes kids mean."

She didn't think he was correct, but she wasn't going to argue with him. It didn't matter anyway. She wasn't a kid anymore. She was an adult, and Gabriel was apparently attracted to her. He'd said he'd been interested in her from the moment he'd met her, and the only information he'd had at that time had been her hair and skin.

"I'm going to tell you you're pretty every day of your life, Eden. Because it's true. And if you argue with me, I'll follow up my compliment with a spanking until you believe me."

She swallowed hard as she stared at him. Was he serious? "You're going to spank me until I think I'm pretty?"

"Yep."

"That seems a little unconventional," she pointed out.

He chuckled. "Maybe, but I bet it will work."

She gave him a small smile. Every time she started to feel bad, or tears welled up again, he said just the right things to make her smile again. He was good at this Daddying business.

Her chest tightened when he stood and kissed her forehead. "Sleep, Little one. I'll be right outside in the living room."

"On the couch? It didn't look long enough for you. Maybe you should stay here." She glanced at the other side of the bed.

"The couch will be just fine. I'll sleep on my side and bend my knees."

She giggled at the visual. "That's silly. I can't kick you out of your bed." Grasping at straws, she added, "Plus, what if I wake up scared in a strange place?"

He chuckled again, his chest shaking. "Do you think that might happen, Little one?"

She nodded, keeping her expression serious. "Or I might have nightmares."

She loved the way his chest rumbled with his laughter. He kissed her forehead again. "If I stayed in here, there would be no sleeping, Little girl. So, you need to slide down under the covers, curl up with Coco, and go to sleep. I'll be right outside the door if you need me."

She found herself pouting as he left the room. Once again, he didn't shut the door all the way. He left it ajar. A few minutes later, she could hear him talking and knew he would be talking to Atlas.

Even though she'd had a very traumatic evening, one of the worst, she found herself feeling safer and more content than she'd felt in a very long time. Two things made that possible. One, nothing bad could possibly happen to her from here inside the MC compound. And two, she did not have to get up tomorrow morning at the crack of dawn to be at work.

Of course, that second fact was a mixed blessing. Not having to be at work also meant she wouldn't have a paycheck. Not having a paycheck meant she wouldn't be able to pay the rent.

Gabriel had insisted she could stay here, but that seemed so unrealistic. He barely knew her. When he got to know her better, he might not like her.

She certainly liked him. A lot. More than she could remember ever liking a man before. And she really liked that she could hear his muffled voice in the other room. It soothed her and allowed her to close her eyes. She could feel herself fading.

Gabriel will protect me.

CHAPTER
FOUR

Gabriel hadn't been kidding about the couch. The only position he could get comfortable in was on his side. Just the one side. His legs were too long to stretch out on his back, and his body was too bulky to face the cushions. After a few hours of tossing, he dragged his blanket to the floor and stretched out.

Lord knew he'd certainly slept in worse conditions when he'd been stationed overseas with the Army. He'd had many uncomfortable nights far worse than this one when he'd been in combat zones.

The sun wasn't up yet when he gave up after a few hours of sleep. The first thing he needed to do was contact his boss. Bensen was the head of the Veterans PTSD Hotline where Gabriel worked. Gabriel was the scheduler, and he didn't have a shift of his own today, but he nearly always made himself available if they needed him, and it was apparent Gabriel would need a few days to get things sorted out with Eden.

He sent a quick email to Bensen and slipped out of his suite to see if anyone else was up. He was going to need some help this morning.

Hearing voices coming from the main kitchen, he was

pleasantly surprised to find both the club president and the enforcer pouring coffee. Steele and Kade would be the most helpful in dealing with his predicament.

Kade passed Gabriel the mug of coffee he'd just poured. "You look like you could use this. Who was the Little girl you came in with last night?" Kade had been on the sofa with his Little, Remi, watching cartoons, but he'd been kind enough to do nothing more than nod.

Steele nodded. "Talon and Bear told me they saw you come in with a Little."

Gabriel sighed. "Her name's Eden. She's a friend of Carlee's from the diner. She had a very frightening incident last night at work. Four of the Devil's Jesters were there. They harassed her verbally and physically. When her boss chose to yell at her instead of supporting her, she walked out the door. She called Carlee. Atlas called me. I went and got her."

Steele ran a hand over his head. "Shit. I've heard the Devil's Jesters have been hanging around more in Shadowridge lately. They've been spotted all over the place. I hope you made her stay here last night."

Gabriel nodded. "Of course I did."

Kade lifted a brow. "Are you planning to make her stay here again tonight?"

"Yep." Gabriel took a sip of the strong coffee.

"And after that?" Kade asked, smirking.

"She's mine," Gabriel admitted. "And I'm going to need some help."

Steele nodded. "Sounds like it. I'm free this morning. Let me round up a few others. I saw Talon a few minutes ago. And I think Bear is around. What are you thinking?"

Gabriel set his mug on the counter. "I could use a bit of muscle to go talk to Marv at the diner. I'd like to do that ASAP. Eden left her purse when she ran out. She'll need me to get it. I'd also like to exchange a few choice words with that slimeball."

Kade rubbed his forehead. "I can go with you, too. Between you, me, Steele, and Talon, I think we'll have enough muscle to intimidate that asshole."

"Thank you. It might be better to leave Bear here with Eden. He can keep her entertained with pancakes."

Suddenly, Bear rounded the corner. "Who needs to be entertained with pancakes?" he asked, his expression serious.

"Gabriel's found himself a Little, and she's in a spot of trouble."

Bear winced. "I'm sorry to hear that. I'll be happy to make the Little girl all the pancakes she can eat while you go slay dragons. If she's nervous, I'll set her up with some cartoons and a sippy cup of chocolate milk after I feed her. I've never had a Little turn down my chocolate milk."

"Appreciate it," Gabriel said with a nod.

"I'll wake Remi and have her join Eden," Kade said.

"Thank you." Gabriel was lucky to have so many brothers have his back no matter what hour of the day or night. Damn, he loved his family. "Hopefully, it won't take us too long to put the fear of God in that smarmy diner manager. After that, I'll want to take Eden to her apartment to pick up some of her things."

"If she had an altercation with the Devil's Jesters, you don't want to go to her apartment without backup either," Steele pointed out.

Gabriel ran a hand through his hair. "That's my thinking, too."

"Perhaps we could go straight there after we hit the diner," Kade suggested.

"I doubt Eden is going to go for that. Even though I made it clear last night that this is her home now, I'm certain she didn't believe me. She's going to wake up wanting to go home. I sense a strong need to be independent in her. It's going to take some cajoling to convince her that even Little girls, who are fully capable of being independent, need a Daddy to lean on sometimes."

"Ain't that the truth," Kade grumbled.

Gabriel picked up his mug. "I better get back to her in case she wakes up. Can we leave in an hour?"

Everyone nodded.

"I'll find Talon," Steele said.

Gabriel stopped by the supply closet to grab some things for Eden before he hurried back to his suite, set his coffee on the counter, and quietly opened the door to the bedroom. He hated to wake her if she was sound asleep. The Little girl needed her rest. She had bags under her eyes. He suspected she hadn't had a good night's rest in a long time.

His heart did a little flip as the light from the living room streamed into his bedroom to illuminate his Little girl. She was curled in a tight ball with Coco clutched against her chest. But what nearly brought him to his knees was the fact that she had her thumb in her mouth.

She was precious with that riot of curls spread out on his pillow and her creamy white cheek begging him to kiss it. At some point, the covers had slid off her, and instead of pulling them back up, she'd tucked her entire legs up into his T-shirt. Only her adorable little feet were visible.

He nearly stopped breathing as he stood over her, watching her rhythmically suck her thumb. Did she know she was a thumb sucker?

Based on what he'd gathered from her last night, she hadn't known Littles were a real thing until Carlee had gotten together with Atlas. And though she'd explored a bit, she hadn't fully grasped her own need for a Daddy.

Damn, he hated to wake her. He set the clothes he'd chosen for her on the end of the bed before gently picking up a ringlet and twirling it between his fingers. Her hair had been damp when she'd gone to bed. He wondered if she normally used some sort of product in it after she washed it. His own hair was getting a bit long, and it was nearly as curly as hers, so he had some relaxers under the sink, but he hadn't thought to offer them to her.

He had a lot to learn about this precious Little girl who'd popped into his life without warning. He was certainly unprepared. He had nothing in his suite for a Little. Thank goodness for the supply closet. He would need to do some shopping later this afternoon.

Eden's pretty green eyes slowly opened and then went wide. A second later, she jerked her thumb out of her mouth as her cheeks turned dark pink. "How long have you been watching me?" she whispered.

"Only a minute, Little one. I hated to wake you, but I didn't want to leave the compound and risk you waking up alone and scared."

She pulled her legs out of his shirt and pushed up to sit, tugging the hem down her thighs. "Oh. Right. You probably have to get to work or something. I'll just get an Uber to take me home and get out of your way."

As she started to ease off the side of the bed, he set a hand on her thigh and stopped her. It was impossible to ignore how smooth her skin was. He hadn't been wrong about that. He was looking forward to kissing her right where his palm now rested.

"Eden, look at Daddy."

Her breath hitched as she met his gaze.

He lowered to sit on the bed next to her legs, keeping his large palm on her thigh. "I'm not going to work, Little one. I work from home, remember? My office is in the spare room."

"Oh, right." She brushed her hair out of her face, but it fell right back down around her cheeks. "What do you do?"

"I manage a PTSD hotline for Veterans. I'm a counselor."

Her eyes went wide. "Really? That's...a really important job."

"Yes, it is. I don't work regular shifts. I handle the scheduling and fill in on the hotline when needed. I don't have to work today."

"Where are you going then?" she asked.

"Some of my brothers and I are going to go talk to Marv and get your purse from the diner."

Her jaw dropped. "You don't have to do that. I can just stop by there later or something."

He moved his hand and set it down on the other side of her hip, putting his face much closer to hers. "Eden, you are never going back there again. It's not safe. I wouldn't send any Little girl to that diner. Your boss is a world-class asshole. You will stay right here and let Daddy handle things."

"I could go back to my apartment at least and wait for you there," she proposed. *Stubborn girl.*

He shook his head. "Little girl, I can't impress this upon you enough. That's not safe either. I'd rather you stay here while I get some things from your apartment." He figured he might as well try to convince her of that.

She shook her head. "How would you know what to get me?"

"You could make me a list."

She chewed on her bottom lip. "How long do you think it will be before those guys lose interest in me and I can go back home? I need to find a new job and—"

Gabriel scooped his stubborn Little girl off the bed, rose to his feet, and carried her cradled in his arms to the living room. Even though she squirmed, he had no trouble containing her, and as soon as he was seated in his favorite armchair, he clamped her down with his hands on her hips.

After a moment of her wiggling, he realized she wasn't fighting him so much as trying to get the T-shirt tugged under her bottom. "Gabriel..."

"Listen to me, Eden," he said in as stern a voice as he dared. "I know a lot happened to you last night, and you're not seeing things clearly yet this morning, but the Devil's

Jesters are bad men. They're undoubtedly not pleased with the outcome of your altercation with them."

"But—"

He shook his head. "No buts, Little girl. I need you to obey me. You're not to leave this compound for any reason without me with you. Do you understand?" He hadn't meant to sound so bossy and firm first thing this morning, but she obviously wasn't taking this situation seriously enough for his taste.

She blinked at him, and then the tears welled up. He hated seeing her cry, but he would deal with the tears as long as she was safe.

"Your safety is important to me, Eden. Very important. But it wouldn't matter if you'd never met the Devil's Jesters last night. You met me, too, and you're mine, Little one. Mine to protect. Mine to take care of. Mine to discipline when you don't obey my safety rules."

She swallowed hard. "Do you see me like that because I'm so young?"

He flinched. "No, Eden. I see you like that because my Daddy instinct is to claim you. Your age doesn't matter to me at all. Twenty-six isn't that young. However, I am twenty years older than you. Do you think I'm too old?" He had to ask.

She shook her head vehemently. "No."

"Then, we don't have a problem." He smiled.

She bit her bottom lip so hard he reached up and plucked it free. "Don't do that. I don't like to see you hurt yourself."

"You really want me to stay here?"

"I do." Thank God she seemed to be catching on. "I'll give you all the time in the world to learn to trust me and accept that I'm your Daddy, but while you're figuring that out, you will follow my rules because I need you to be safe. You may not go back to your apartment. You may not go back to the diner. You may not go anywhere."

"How will I get a new job if I don't leave the MC?"

"You won't, Little one. Daddy will take care of your needs.

If working is really important to you, we'll discuss you getting a new job in the future when I'm certain the Devil's Jesters are no longer a threat to your life."

"But…"

Stubborn Little girl was going to have him hopping. "Ladybug, you're about to become intimately acquainted with my palm…"

"But…"

"Eden…" he warned. "Do I need to spank you before breakfast to help you understand who's in charge?"

She gasped and shook her head.

"Good. Now, let's get you dressed so you can go eat breakfast while I go to the diner with some of my brothers. If you give me your address and the key to your apartment, I'll—"

She shook her head. "I promise I'll be good while you go to the diner. I won't complain a single time if you'll take me with you to my apartment afterward."

He'd expected this, so he was prepared to relent. He lifted a brow and gave her a stern look. "I'm going to leave you here with Bear. He makes some mean pancakes. One of the other Little girls, Remi, is here this morning, too. You can play with her while I'm gone. If you're a good girl and don't give Bear any trouble, I'll take you with me after we go to the diner."

She sat up taller and nodded her consent. "I'll be good. I promise."

Damn, she was Little. It was shocking that she'd had no idea until last night. She was stinking adorable.

She was also going to be a handful.

CHAPTER
FIVE

Eden's heart pounded as Gabriel stood her on her feet and led her back into the bedroom.

"Let's get you dressed," he stated.

She hadn't noticed the pile of clothes on the end of the bed until now. "Where did you get clothes?"

"I told you we have a supply closet for every kind of emergency situation. I picked out a few things so you wouldn't have to spend the morning in Daddy's T-shirt, but if you'd rather stay dressed how you are…"

She shook her head as she tugged the material down. It hung way past her butt, but she still felt the need to pull on it since she wasn't wearing any underwear.

If there was a supply closet, why didn't he take her there to pick out something for herself? "How did you know my sizes?"

He sat on the edge of the bed and lifted a pair of black stretchy leggings, red socks, and a cute black T-shirt with a ladybug on the front.

She got so excited that she stepped closer. "That's a ladybug. I love ladybugs. How did you know?"

He grinned. "I had no idea. It was a coincidence." He set

those down and picked up an unopened packet of panties next. There were three pairs inside. Pastel colors. They had little bows on them. In fact, they looked exactly like what a four-year-old would wear but in an adult size. "I bet these will fit you fine." He opened them and held out all three. "Which color do you want to wear?"

She pointed at the pink pair, but when she tried to take them from him, he pulled them out of her grasp. Next, he snagged her hand and hauled her closer before tipping her head back with his fingers under her chin. "Do you remember what I said last night about taking care of you in all ways, Little one?"

She flushed as she stared at him. Did he mean to dress her? God, yes, he did. She wasn't sure how she felt about that, but her body betrayed her as she watched his face. Her nipples tightened and then wetness gathered between her legs.

The thought of Gabriel seeing her naked excited her for some reason. And that embarrassed her. She was still pondering this dilemma when he gently pulled her between his legs and hugged her hips with his knees.

She shivered as he ran his hands up her bare arms before cupping her face and leaning in closer. "Can you be brave for me, Ladybug?"

She couldn't keep from smiling at him calling her Ladybug. It was so sweet. She felt herself softening under his intense gaze. His brows were furrowed, but his look was one of concern.

She grabbed his thighs to steady herself. They were solid. He was so muscly and serious. Did those adjectives even go together? "Uh, you want to see me naked?"

"I want to take care of you in every way, and that will involve me seeing your body, Eden. For this morning, my only plan is to pull this shirt off you and put these clothes on you so you can go have breakfast."

She worried her bottom lip for a moment. She was pretty

shy about her body. She'd only had a few boyfriends, and none of them had seemed wowed by her, so she'd grown even more self-conscious as an adult than she'd been as a child.

Gabriel seemed pretty adamant that he intended to be her Daddy, which was overwhelming since she'd met him just last night. If she weighed the pros and cons, she thought letting him see her might not be a bad idea. If he didn't find her attractive, she would see it in his reaction, which would put a period at the end of this oddly rushed relationship sentence.

"'Kay," she whispered.

"Good girl." He set her back a few inches, lifted the T-shirt over her head, and then twisted to grab the pink panties. When he turned back to face her, he slid off the bed and squatted in front of her. "Hold Daddy's shoulders, Ladybug."

She held her breath, not sure she could lift the foot he was tapping. Even gripping his shoulders wasn't going to keep her from swaying. She was so unnerved standing in front of him naked.

He lifted his gaze to hers and then jerked it down to her body. For long seconds, he let his gaze roam up and down her frame before swallowing. "Eden..." His voice was husky.

"I told you I'm not attractive," she blurted. Why hadn't he listened to her?

His eyes went wide a second before he grabbed her hips, rose to his feet, lifted her off the floor, and turned to lie her on the bed. He dropped his hands alongside her and held her gaze. He looked...angry. "What did I say about talking negatively about yourself?"

She sniffled. Her bottom lip was trembling, and she felt so exposed. Why couldn't he just let her get dressed?

"Listen to me, Little girl. I'm going to give you this one last pass with regard to how you view yourself. The next time you say something derisive about your body, I will take you over my knee and spank your bare bottom until you learn a lesson."

She couldn't breathe. He was serious.

"Now, another thing. Besides the fact that I won't tolerate you thinking or speaking ill of yourself, you're dead wrong. I was trying hard not to look so you wouldn't be uncomfortable with me dressing you this morning, but when you hesitated, I had no choice. You knocked the wind out of my lungs. You're the most beautiful woman I've ever set eyes on. Every inch of you. My cock is so hard right now I'm going to need a cold shower before we can head to the kitchen."

She was stunned. Were his arms shaking? Was he being truthful? He didn't seem like the sort of man who would lie to a woman. Plus, if he wanted to fib, he could have just said he thought she was fine or cute. He wouldn't have needed an elaborate speech.

"Your skin is fucking perfection. Your pink little nipples make my mouth water. Your breasts are the exact handful I look forward to worshipping with my palms and my tongue. That little dip of your tummy before the flare of your hips makes me want to circle your waist and never let you go. I cannot wait to flip you over and spank your white bottom, so I can watch it turn pink from my palm."

She gasped. That last part made her squirm. Why did the thought of him spanking her make her nipples hard? Maybe it was simply the cool air in the room. But that didn't explain the throbbing sensation between her legs.

If he was saying all that just to humor her, he was doing a fine job convincing her. She believed him well enough for tears to form in her eyes. No one had ever said such kind things to her about her looks.

"Now, we'll address this subject again later. Right now, I need to put these clothes on you before I change my mind and decide I'd rather suck those precious little nipples until you writhe before dipping my face lower and thrusting my tongue into your pussy until you scream. But mark my words, Little girl, that will happen soon, and Daddy is going to enjoy every moment of it."

Her heart was racing, and so was her mind.

"Repeat after me: I'm beautiful and perfect just the way I am."

She licked her lips.

"Say it, Ladybug."

It seemed silly, but he was insistent. "I'm beautiful and perfect just the way I am," she whispered.

"Good girl." He righted himself, grabbed the panties, and pulled them up her legs while she lay on the bed in front of him.

Her breath hitched with embarrassment when his fingers grazed the curls covering her sex. "I…"

"You what, Ladybug?"

"I guess most girls shave…down there. I just…well, I mean no one… It's been a while since… I wasn't expecting…" Damn, it was hard to spit that all out, plus it sounded ridiculous out loud. Why was she making excuses for her pubic hair?

He gave her a slow smile. "Eden, I do not care one way or the other about the hair on your pussy. If you like it that way, keep it. If you want to shave it, that's okay, too. If you want *me* to shave it, I'm also good with that. It's your choice. The only person you need to please is you. Do what makes you feel best about yourself."

She gasped. Did he just say he would shave it?

He chuckled. "You heard me." He pulled the black leggings up her legs next and settled them over her hips before threading their fingers together and helping her sit upright.

Her head was spinning as he picked up the ladybug shirt. "Arms up, Little one."

She lifted her arms and let him put the shirt on before realizing she wasn't wearing a bra. "I need a bra."

He tugged the shirt down to her hips and then kissed her forehead. "Now *that* I might take issue with. If you want to wear a bra when you're someplace in public in your adult headspace, that's fine. But here in the compound, you don't need one. Trust me on this. You'll feel Littler without a bra."

She tugged on the shirt. It wasn't like her boobs were so big they needed support, but it felt funny not wearing a bra. She'd been wearing one since she'd turned twelve. And she certainly hadn't needed one that year.

While she was still sitting on the edge of the bed, Gabriel put the red socks on her. "There. Did I do a good job?"

She couldn't help but giggle. Now that she was dressed, she felt lighter.

He lifted her off the bed and set her on her feet. "How do you want Daddy to fix your hair? I grabbed a cute pair of ladybug hair baubles if you want me to put your curls up in pigtails." He snagged them from the foot of the bed. They'd been under the clothes.

She took them from him. "Those are so cute." She really wanted to wear them, but pigtails? "Aren't I kind of old for pigtails?"

He gasped dramatically and put a hand over his heart. "No one is too old for pigtails."

She giggled again. "My hair is so curly they would stand out to here." She held her hands out as far as she could reach.

"I think you're exaggerating, but I could do braids if you'd rather." He took her hand and led her to the attached bath, where he grabbed a comb, parted her hair down the middle, and proceeded to braid one side as if he'd done so every day of her life. That's how efficient he was, and it raised a question she'd been wondering. "How many Little girls have you had?"

"You're the first, Ladybug. I've waited a long time to meet you. My brothers who have Littles told me I would know when I met the right one, and they were right. I certainly did."

That was still a bit hard to fathom, even though she secretly felt like he'd been sent by God. It still scared her. This was happening too fast. "Why do you know how to braid hair so well then?" she asked as he finished the first one and took the ladybug from her hand to secure the end.

"Oh. That's simple. There are a lot of Little girls around here, Ladybug. It seems like another one of my brothers finds the perfect woman for him every damn day lately. Steele has Ivy. Kade has Remi. Atlas has Carlee. Doc has Harper. It's like an epidemic." He chuckled. "Sometimes, a Little girl's Daddy isn't around when she needs her hair done. I'm getting pretty good at it."

She stared at his reflection in the mirror as he continued, hand over hand, making the perfect braid. Maybe she should feel jealous that he did this to other men's girlfriends, but instead, she got the sense they were like a family. Gabriel was like an uncle to those other women. She suddenly longed to be a member of this club—not the MC exactly, but the Daddy club. Could she really be this lucky?

"There," he declared as he fastened the second ladybug. "Ready to go meet Bear and have some pancakes?"

The mention made her remember that he was going to leave, and the reason made her nervous. What if something happened to him because of her? She lowered her gaze and twined her fingers together. "I should've just *told* them..." she murmured, mostly to herself.

"Told who what, Ladybug?" he asked as he lifted her chin.

"It doesn't matter." Not now. The damage was done now.

He sat on the toilet seat and brought her between his legs again. He seemed to like this position. It put them eye to eye. She liked it, too. "Explain what you meant, Eden. Told who what?"

"Those men. The Devil's Jesters. If I wasn't so uptight and such a prude, I could've laughed and shook them off or made a joke and—"

His grip on her hips tightened. "Eden..." His voice was filled with warning. "And told them what?"

She lowered her face. "That the carpet does match the drapes," she whispered.

His breath hitched, and his fingers dug into her butt cheeks before he seemed to realize he was holding her too tightly and loosened his hands. "No. Jesus. Eden. No. What those men said was incredibly inappropriate, rude, distasteful, offensive, sexually harassing, and about a dozen other things. No one should ever talk to a woman that way. Besides, what do you think would've happened if you'd laughed and pretended like it hadn't bothered you? What if you'd answered their question?"

She shrugged. A lot of possibilities ran through her mind. None of them were pretty.

"I know. They would've felt empowered to continue harassing you until you got off work. Then they would've followed you home, and I don't even want to think how that would've gone."

She sighed. He was right. "But at least you wouldn't be going to the diner to face Marv and get my purse back. He has probably put it in the dumpster by now."

"And I've told you I'm not afraid of Marv. If he touched your purse, I will call the police and file a report. I bet he won't like the cops pulling up during business hours."

Her eyes went wide. "Gabriel, he's going to be furious. I'll never be able to leave this compound again if you go over there. My purse isn't worth it. I'll just get a new ID from the state. I'll tell them I lost it. It's not like I had a lot of cash or a credit card or anything. It's just a purse."

"Doesn't matter what's in it, Ladybug. It's yours. And as I've pointed out before, you have way bigger problems than Marv. You can't leave this compound unattended until I can ensure those Jester assholes aren't going to come after you."

She started trembling. He was right. "I really made a mess of things."

He gave her hips a shake. "You did not do anything wrong,

Eden. Nothing. Five men sexually harassed you. That's not your fault. I'm going to take care of it."

She knew when he said five, he was including Marv. He was right. Marv hadn't stood up for her or asked the men to leave or even apologize. Marv had insinuated everything had been her fault and taken their side. He was no better.

"You won't do anything that would get you in trouble, right?" The thought of him getting arrested because of her made her chest tighten. For one thing, she didn't want to be such a burden, but more importantly, she wanted him to come back here so she could spend more time with him and see if this odd thing between them could possibly be real.

"No, Ladybug. I promise I'll be fine. I may want to throw a few punches, but I won't actually do so."

"Okay." She didn't know him well enough to be certain he wouldn't get violent. He didn't seem violent. He'd been nothing but caring and gentle with her. But he was in a motorcycle club. He did wear an intimidating vest. He had tattoos, a beard, and hair long enough that he'd pulled it into a bun. If she'd met him on the street, he would have intimidated her.

"Let's get you to the kitchen. I'm sure my brothers are waiting for me."

CHAPTER
SIX

As Gabriel led his Little girl—and she was most definitely his Little girl—out of the bathroom, he stopped her. "We haven't had time to go over any rules yet, Ladybug, but I'm going to give you one right now. No running in the clubhouse, especially not in socked feet. Got it?"

Her cheeks turned pink as she stared at him with those wide eyes. "Gabriel, I'm an adult."

He stopped midway through the bedroom to face her and cup her cheeks. "Ladybug, Little girls like you have no choice but to step in and out of two different mindsets. Sometimes, you will have to put your adult hat on and take care of adult business. That's just life. If you decide you want to get another job and work somewhere, you will, of course, need to set your Little aside while you're out in the world. However, most of the time when you're here in the compound or any other safe place with me, you'll get used to staying in your Little space, and Little girls need structure and rules. One of those is no running in the building. Your feet might slide out from under you, and you could hit your noggin on the floor. Then I'd have to take you to Doc and get the all-clear from him before I can spank your naughty bottom to remind you of the rules."

The shudder that shook her slight frame made him want to sweep her off the floor, carry her to the armchair in the living room, and cradle her in his arms.

"Is Doc one of your brothers? You mentioned him before."

"Yep. He was a medic in the Army. Now, he's a medic for the local fire department in town. He takes care of minor booboos when naughty Little girls get hurt."

"I could get hurt without being naughty," she countered.

Damn, she was cute and growing cuter as she got more comfortable with him, enough so that she was able to bring out her sassy side. "This is true, but in my experience, lately, most of the Little girls scampering around here get hurt more often than not when they're up to naughty shenanigans."

She giggled. "That's silly."

"You'll see." He grabbed her hand and continued toward the door to the main hallway.

She tugged on his hand at the last moment. "Wait. Are you expecting me to pretend to be your Little girl when we leave this room?"

Gabriel stopped, reminding himself she was new to the lifestyle and to being his. "Ladybug, all of my brother's girlfriends are Little. There's no pretending. They don't hide it inside the compound. Any time two or more of them are here, they play together, laugh together, eat together, and cause mischief together. You will fit right in. I promise."

"I don't know…" She chewed on her bottom lip as she pondered his suggestion.

"You'll see—no need to fret. Just be yourself, and you'll be fine. Now, any other concerns? I'm starting to think I need to toss you over my shoulder and carry you out of here, or we'll never make it to the kitchen."

Her pretty green eyes went wide again. "You wouldn't dare."

Gabriel bent at the waist, tucked his shoulder into her tummy, and lifted her right off the floor. He kept one hand firmly across her bottom as she squirmed and squealed. "Put me down!"

He gave her bottom a quick swat. "Be good."

She gasped and stopped fighting him as she reached back with one hand to rub her bottom. "Owie."

Not Little, my ass.

Gabriel held on tight as he carried her down the hall, through the common area, and into the kitchen. He loved the way she squirmed in his grip, but he didn't set her down until he reached the table, where he lowered her into a chair.

Remi was already there, seated in the chair next to the one Gabriel chose for Eden, and she was giggling.

Eden's cheeks were pink as she smoothed her shirt down where it had ridden up to expose her tummy.

"You must be Eden," Remi said, holding out a hand. The Little stinker was dressed in her usual goth style with dark eyeliner, black lipstick, and a black-and-white dress with a tutu, which stuck out all around her.

Eden tentatively shook Remi's hand.

"Carlee has talked about you," Remi continued. "And my Daddy said we could play together this morning. Do you like puzzles?"

Gabriel watched Eden closely. Remi was so sweet to pull Eden into her world so seamlessly.

Steele, Kade, and Talon were standing behind the girls drinking coffee. They had obviously been waiting for Gabriel, who'd taken longer than he'd expected to get Eden ready to face everyone this morning.

"I like puzzles," Eden murmured in a shy voice. Gabriel didn't think she would be shy once she got to know everyone, but it was reasonable for her to be a bit overwhelmed this morning. All of this was new to her.

Bear was at the stove, and the room smelled like bacon. He

wiped his hands on a towel and set a huge palm on top of Eden's head, causing her to tip her head back. He grinned at her. "Welcome to the family, Little one. I'm Bear. I hope you like pancakes."

She smiled at him. "I love pancakes."

"Do you want chocolate chips in yours?"

Her eyes widened, and Gabriel knew Bear had won her over. "I love chocolate chips."

Steele chuckled. "Ivy will join you girls in a few minutes. I'm glad I'll be gone for a while. There's going to be a collective sugar high going on."

As Bear returned to the stove, Gabriel leaned over Eden and cupped her chin. "Will you be okay for a while?"

Remi chuckled in a mischievous tone. "Don't you worry. I'll teach her how to put on black eyeliner and smokey eyeshadow. After that, we'll talk about what tattoos she wants and maybe about piercing her eyebrows or perhaps her lip."

Gabriel's chest tightened, and he shot Remi a look.

She giggled. "Just kidding, but the look on your face was totally worth it."

Kade closed the distance, set a hand on Remi's neck, and used the other to pull her head back by the ponytail. "Do you need me to spank you before breakfast, naughty girl?"

She squirmed in her seat. "No, Daddy. I was just joking around with Uncle Gabriel. We'll be good. I promise."

"Let's go," Gabriel stated. He wanted to get this confrontation with Marv over with as soon as possible.

Doc wandered into the kitchen with his hand wrapped around Harper. Their relationship was new, and Harper was still a bit skittish. She was on the shyer side. Maybe her presence would be good for Eden.

"Ah, I heard there was a new Little girl in the compound." He lifted Harper onto a chair across from Eden and Remi. At the same time, Ivy rushed into the room to join everyone.

Introductions went all around again.

Gabriel squatted down next to Eden. "I won't be long. Be good."

She bit into her lower lip and nodded. Her pretty cheeks were hot pink.

He kissed her forehead and hurried out of the room with the others. He hated leaving her, but this was necessary, and she was in good hands now with both Doc and Bear in the kitchen.

Five minutes later, he, Steele, Kade, and Talon were on their bikes, pulling out of the compound's front gate.

CHAPTER
SEVEN

Overwhelmed was too mild a term for how Eden felt sitting at this table surrounded by strangers. The women were super nice, and she could tell they were fun, but she felt out of body.

So much had happened in the last ten hours her head was spinning. It was also weird that the two men in the room were waiting on the four women, and yet none of the women batted an eye. It was clear they were used to this treatment.

Doc took drink orders and filled sippy cups with juice and milk while Bear dished up scrambled eggs, bacon, and pancakes into brightly-colored, compartmented plastic plates.

Harper seemed a bit quieter than the other two women. She looked slightly overwhelmed, like Eden felt. Maybe she was shy, or maybe she was new here, too.

Eden had never been around so many people. She'd been an only child and had grown up without much extended family. It was hard to be nervous, though, because everyone was so kind, and the food was delicious.

After one bite of the chocolate chip pancakes dripping with syrup, she turned to Bear. "Thank you. These are so good."

"You're welcome, Little one. Let me know if you need more."

Remi leaned in conspiratorially. "I told Eden we could do a puzzle after breakfast while the Daddies are gone, but maybe we should think of something mischievous instead." She giggled.

Eden's breath hitched. She sure wished Carlee were here. She'd be far more comfortable if she knew at least one person. What sort of mischief was Remi talking about?

"Girls..." Doc admonished in a deep voice. "I can hear you, you know. I'm standing right here. How about you do something that won't get you into trouble this morning? Eden just got here last night. I doubt she's ready to have her bottom spanked in front of everyone."

Eden squeezed her thighs together and clenched her butt cheeks. It seemed like all these people ever talked about was getting spanked. Apparently, it was a huge part of the lifestyle, and it seemed these women liked that aspect.

It was mindboggling because Eden had never considered such a concept before Gabriel had threatened to spank her several times. When he'd done so, she'd found herself feeling curious and a bit turned on, but she had no interest in getting spanked by someone other than Gabriel. That was for sure.

Remi sighed.

"We'll be good, Daddy," Harper said softly.

Ivy groaned. "If we must. But just this morning. No promises for later today."

Doc chuckled and shook his head.

Yeah, this dynamic was bizarre. Eden was stunned.

When they were finished eating, Bear and Doc came over with washcloths and wiped all their mouths and fingers before shooing them toward the common area.

"Behave," Bear growled, but his tone held no weight. He was all bluff and clearly loved doting on the women.

Eden followed the others into a space off the common area filled with books, games, and toys.

Ivy clapped her hands together. "How about if we do a puzzle this morning so Eden doesn't get her bottom spanked, and then we can plot mischief when the Daddies are back...?" She lifted up a moderately difficult puzzle covered with colorful balloons.

"Sounds good," Remi said as she sat at the game table.

Eden joined them, grateful they didn't intend to misbehave. She couldn't quite wrap her head around that concept, yet these women seemed to be rubbing their hands together, plotting ways to get into trouble.

As she took her seat, she squirmed again. Gabriel had given her one swat while she'd been over his shoulder. It had startled her. It had also reverberated through her body in an odd way. *Hmmm.*

The puzzle was half done when Eden looked up to see Carlee running toward her. Eden pushed her chair back and raced around the table to throw herself at her friend. They hugged and rocked for several seconds before releasing each other.

It wasn't that Eden and Carlee had ever been best friends. It was more that they'd had a common hatred for their jobs at the diner and Marv in particular. Eden had been so jealous the day Atlas had come in and waltzed Carlee right out the door without looking back.

It would seem that another member of the Shadowridge Guardians had stepped up to the plate to extricate a woman from that diner. Gabriel was her savior, but was he really her Daddy?

"What are you doing here?" she asked Carlee. "I thought

you were out of town for the weekend. Gabriel said he would have you call me this morning."

"I couldn't sleep a wink last night, and Daddy knew I wasn't going to enjoy myself, so we got up early and headed back."

"Oh. I'm so sorry. I didn't mean to cut your trip short."

Carlee shrugged. "It's okay. We'll do it again another time. You're more important than a weekend away." She grabbed Eden's hand and led her to a sofa in the common area. "Tell me everything."

Eden looked around. No one was nearby, but most of what she wanted to discuss with Carlee had nothing to do with what had happened last night at work and everything to do with the feelings Gabriel was bringing out in her.

Carlee must have read her mind because she nodded. "Let's go to my suite." She glanced at the other women. "We'll be back in a few."

"Excellent," Remi exclaimed. "Tell Eden what it means to be naughty so we can get into some mischief this afternoon." She grinned widely.

Carlee laughed. "Okay."

When she turned around to drag Eden out of the room by the hand, Atlas stopped her with a hand on her shoulder. "You okay, Eden?"

Eden nodded, her cheeks heating. She'd met Atlas several times but still felt awkward around him.

Carlee gave him a smile. "We're going to go to our suite to talk for a bit, so we'll have some privacy."

"Okay, Baby girl. Text me if you need anything. I'm going to head into town and grab a few things from my office." He kissed her. Not a quick peck, but not a full-on make-out session, either. Something in between. It was powerful and possessive and made Eden fidget as she watched. "Be good," he murmured against Carlee's lips.

"I will, Daddy," she said before moving toward the hallway, still gripping Eden's hand. She'd never let go.

The suite they entered was across the hall from Gabriel's. The layout was almost identical. Carlee led Eden to the couch and plopped down. "I had to do a doubletake when I saw you sitting at the table. You're...Little." She grinned and bounced a bit.

Eden lowered to sit beside her friend, glancing down at her clothes. The braids would have given Carlee that impression. "I don't know," she murmured. "Gabriel did this." She tugged on her braids and then plucked her shirt.

"You look so cute. I love it."

When Carlee curled her legs under her, so did Eden, feeling comfortable and more relaxed than she had all morning.

"I heard about what Marv did from Atlas. I won't make you rehash that part. I'm sorry about those mean men who were tormenting you, too. Tell me what happened with Gabriel," she encouraged.

Eden was glad because she didn't want to think about the Devil's Jesters. She wanted to work out what was happening between her and Gabriel. "He's so bossy."

Carlee laughed. "All Daddies are bossy."

"Yeah, I see that. I've met several this morning."

"So...you slept here last night?"

"Yeah. Alone. Gabriel insisted on me taking his bed. He slept on the couch. I felt bad, but he insisted."

"Very gentlemanly of him," Carlee said. "And then what?"

Eden drew in a breath and rehashed everything that had happened that morning, not leaving out any details, including the part about him stripping her naked, putting clothes on her, and fixing her hair.

Carlee set the back of her hand over her forehead and leaned back in a dramatic swoon.

Eden couldn't keep from giggling. "You're not supposed to

be laughing. You're supposed to be helping me understand this craziness."

Carlee righted herself. "What's to understand? Do you like him?"

Eden thought about that for a second. "Yes. I mean, how could I not? He's all dominant and growly and bossy, and it's hot. What I don't understand is why *he* likes *me*."

Carlee's eyes went wide. "What are you talking about? How could he *not* like you? You're so cute and pretty and sweet and fun. I bet he fell for your pretty hair and freckles the moment he saw you. I wish I had that hair."

Eden gasped, and then she tugged on one of the braids. "This mess? Nobody wants this hair. I've spent my whole life wishing I had been born in a different body."

Carlee frowned. "Why? It's so pretty. I don't know how you've managed to remain single for so long."

Eden cringed as the words she'd heard from her classmates started ringing in her head all over again.

Carrot top, carrot top.

Oh, girl, you're blinding me. Turn down the lights.

Is your head on fire?

Did you get your finger stuck in a socket?

Why don't you shave that off and get a wig, fire girl?

Are you a vampire? That skin is so white it hurts my eyes.

Eden squeezed her eyes closed and covered her ears as if she could block out the mean words.

"Hey." Carlee scooted closer and set a hand on Eden's back. "Are you okay?"

Eden tried to relax her body, eventually lowering her hands and staring at her lap.

"You better not let Gabriel hear you speaking negatively about yourself. He'll take you over his knee so fast you won't have to wonder what it feels like to get spanked any longer."

Eden cringed. "I already got that lecture from him twice."

Carlee rubbed her back. "I'm not surprised. These Daddy

types get pretty prickly when a Little talks down about herself."

Eden lifted her head. "Do you really think he could like me?"

"I'm certain you would not be sitting here wearing that adorable ladybug outfit if he didn't. And where is he now?" She lifted a brow.

Eden knew Carlee was well aware of where Gabriel was. She was trying to make a point. Eden sighed. "He went to talk to Marv. I wish he hadn't."

Carlee smiled. "These Daddies are fierce protectors, too. They don't take kindly to anyone being mean to any of their Littles. He'd do the same thing for me or any one of us. Hell, he'd do it for a stranger if she needed help."

"That's me. I'm that stranger. He came in the dark without hesitation to pick me up on the side of the road because Atlas asked him to. That doesn't mean he likes me."

Carlee narrowed her gaze. "You know that's not true. He may have gone to get you because Atlas asked him to, but he wouldn't have tucked you into his bed and dressed you this morning if he wasn't interested in you."

Eden let her shoulders drop. "Okay."

"Now, how did you manage to spend the morning with Remi, Ivy, and Harper and not get into trouble? Usually, when two or more of us are gathered, Operation Shenanigans goes into effect."

Eden giggled. "Oh, they tried. I think they only held back because I was so shocked and confused."

Carlee clapped her hands together. "Then it's time to find us some trouble. Let's go join the others. I bet they have ideas." She jumped to her feet. "It will take your mind off what's happening at the diner."

Eden slowly rose. "So, let me get this straight. You all misbehave on purpose because you like getting your bottoms spanked?"

"Absolutely."

Eden shook her head. "It makes no sense. Doesn't it hurt?"

"Yep. It hurts so good. You'll see." Carlee grabbed her hand. "Trust me."

"But Doc and Bear are the only ones in the compound right now. Would they spank all of us? I don't think I'd want someone else besides Gabriel to spank me."

"Sometimes, other Daddies spank a Little, but only if that's something she likes and has agreed to. Lots of Littles prefer to be disciplined by only their own Daddies. There's no way someone else would spank you this early in your relationship. If all five of us get into trouble, Doc and Bear will make us wait for the others to return to punish us."

"How naughty are we talking?" Eden asked. This concept was baffling.

"Don't worry. We never do anything dangerous. Nor do we do anything that would cause permanent destruction to the property. We invent silly things that break minor rules."

Eden slowly smiled as she started to catch on to the idea. It sounded freeing. When was the last time she'd let herself go, relaxed, and created mischief? Maybe never. "I wasn't even naughty as a child," she informed Carlee.

"All the more reason to do so now."

"I don't have shoes," Eden pointed out.

Carlee turned around, dashed into the bedroom, and returned a moment later with a pair of white tennis shoes. "I think we're almost the same size."

Eden sat on the couch to put them on.

When she was ready, Carlee opened the door and took off, skipping toward the common area.

Eden had to run to keep up with her friend.

"Girls!" Bear shouted as they passed him at the entrance to the kitchen. "No running!"

"Sorry, Bear," Carlee said without a glance or even slowing down.

CHAPTER
EIGHT

As soon as they joined the other three girls, everyone stood up from the nearly finished puzzle.

Remi's face lit up. "I smell mischief."

Carlee giggled as she glanced over her shoulder. "What should we do?"

"We could play hide and seek," Ivy suggested. "It always drives the Daddies crazy when they can't find us."

"Oh!" Carlee bounced on her feet. "I have an idea. Let's tell them we're going to go outside to play and then climb in that big tree so they can't find us."

Remi giggled. "You and that tree." She turned to the other girls. "Carlee and I used to hide in that tree when we were kids." She turned back to Carlee. "I don't know if we'll fool anyone."

"Maybe Doc and Bear," Carlee suggested. "They aren't as familiar with my history as Kade and Atlas. They might not think about the tree."

"I don't know about this," Harper whispered. "My bottom still hurts from last night."

Ivy giggled. "Sometimes a spanking on top of a spanking is even better. It stings so good."

Harper rubbed her bottom, wincing.

Eden stared at them all, feeling like she'd slid into another dimension. Five grown women were plotting to get into trouble on purpose with grown men who would then punish them.

Sure, she'd read this in stories, but she'd never imagined it in real life. Apparently, she'd been living in a box.

"Eden? You in?" Carlee asked.

"I guess."

"Harper?"

"Okay…" Harper grumbled, "but next time, I want to just chill and play with my dolls, and somebody better join me."

Eden shifted her attention to Harper. "You have dolls?"

Harper slowly nodded.

"I think that sounds fun. I haven't played with dolls in forever," Eden continued.

Harper smiled at her.

"Come on. Let's go outside before someone comes to check on us," Remi urged.

"Are we even going to tell them we're going out back?" Ivy asked.

"Not if we don't have to," Carlee added. "That will make it even better."

Eden felt invigorated in the strangest way as she followed the other women as they tiptoed out the door that led from the common area to a large outdoor space with grills, swing sets, a sandbox, and the best climbing tree she'd ever seen.

Soft giggling filled the air as they all raced toward the tree.

"Man, this tree is fantastic," Eden said as she grabbed a branch behind Carlee and started to climb. She didn't think she'd ever actually climbed a tree when she'd been a kid. She hadn't had one as cool as this one.

"Remi and I used to hide up here when we were kids. It was so much fun," Carlee told her as they kept climbing. It was so big that all five of them could find a branch several yards off the ground without a problem.

"Girls?"

"Shhh," Ivy whispered. "Bear's coming."

Bear's booming voice could be heard again a moment later as Doc joined him. "I thought they'd come out back."

"They better not have. They didn't even ask for permission," Doc said.

Eden glanced at Harper to find her wincing and rubbing her bottom again. It didn't seem like naughty was something Harper liked to participate in.

"Did you check the suites?" Bear asked.

"Yep. All of them. Those stinkers are up to something. It was brewing all morning. They were itching to create mischief." Doc's voice was jovial, though. He didn't seem to mind.

So interesting. Eden felt herself getting swept into the fun.

Suddenly, the sound of bikes entering the compound made her glance toward the gated entrance. A few minutes later, Gabriel, Steele, Talon, and Kade stepped into sight, joining Doc and Bear.

"What are you doing out here?" Gabriel asked.

"Looking for the girls," Doc responded.

Gabriel's voice hitched as he responded. "What do you mean?" He glanced around.

Bear grumbled. "What he means is those little stinkers are playing hide and seek from us. They were in the library doing a puzzle, and when I went to check on them, they were gone."

Gabriel's chest pumped out as he set his hands on his hips.

Eden felt kind of bad. He looked worried.

"Don't worry," Carlee whispered from nearby. "They're used to this."

That might be, but if Gabriel didn't have a Little girl of his own, he wasn't exactly used to this. She hated making him worry.

"How did those girls manage to convince Eden to join in their shenanigans? She hasn't even been here a full day," Gabriel pointed out.

Eden bit her lip. Her heart was racing.

"Are you kidding?" Kade asked. "Remi and Carlee could easily have talked her into this."

"But Carlee isn't even here. She and Atlas are out of town."

Kade shook his head. "Got a text from Atlas a bit ago. They came back. Carlee was worried about Eden."

Suddenly, another man stepped outside. He was slightly older. Eden hadn't met him yet. "What's this I hear about naughty girls hiding?"

"All five of them," Steele informed him.

"Five?" the man asked.

Talon nodded. "Gabriel met his Little girl last night."

The man chuckled. "And she's already hiding from you?"

Eden held her breath. How much trouble was she going to be in for this stunt?

Gabriel growled. "Peer pressure is powerful."

The other men laughed.

The older man glanced up, his gaze seeming to land directly on Eden. His grin was huge. "Found them."

The rest of the men followed his line of sight.

"Oh, darn," Carlee said. "If Rock hadn't joined them, we would've gotten away with this longer."

"How did he know?" Eden asked.

"He's Atlas and Remi's father. He's well aware of where we kids hid when we were younger," Carlee groaned.

As soon as Rock stepped under the tree, Carlee added, "Meanie."

He chuckled, shook his head, and returned to the clubhouse.

"Remi," Kade called up. "Whose idea was this?"

"Idea for what, Daddy?" she asked all innocently. "We

aren't doing anything. We just wanted to show Eden how cool this old tree is."

"Uh-huh."

Gabriel stared directly at Eden. His brow was furrowed, making him look stern, but the corners of his mouth were turned up slightly. She'd seen that look before. He wasn't angry. He was humored. But he was trying hard to keep from laughing. Thank goodness.

Steele's booming voice was next. "Be sure not to scrape your bottoms on those branches on the way down. Those open wounds will hurt when we make contact with our palms."

Ivy groaned. "Daddy…"

Eden stiffened, but Carlee giggled. "Trust me." She wiggled around sideways and lowered herself to the next branch.

"Easy for you to say," Eden muttered under her breath. "Your Daddy isn't even here right now."

Eden was the last to reach the lowest branch, and she looked down to find Gabriel right beneath her. He held up his hands and grabbed her around the waist as she eased her body in his direction.

As soon as her feet were on the ground, he spun her around and pulled her into his arms so tightly she couldn't breathe. He even lifted her off her feet and held her higher against him.

She squirmed as she tried to inhale. "Gabriel…I need air."

"Mmm. Sorry." He loosened his grip, but he didn't put her down. He leaned her back a few inches and met her gaze. He was grinning. "I guess you had no trouble fitting in with the other Little girls."

She shrugged, still squirming. "Are you going to put me down?"

"Nope." Instead, he slid one arm lower, lifted her legs, and cradled her against him as he turned toward the clubhouse. The others were already being ushered through the door. Eden could hear grumbling and complaints and excuses. It was kind of comical.

"This is a weird dimension I've stepped into," Eden commented.

Gabriel chuckled. "It's going to get weirder when I spank your naughty bottom."

She gasped. "You can't do that. I'm...new, and-and-and all we did was climb a tree. You didn't say I couldn't climb trees. You only said I couldn't run in the house."

"And did you run in the house?" he asked, one brow rising as he continued through the common room toward the hallway where the suites were located.

She stared at him, noticing he was struggling not to laugh. "Do the Daddies always tattle on the Littles?" She knew Bear had probably texted him.

"Yep."

"That's just mean."

"That's how things are when you have a giant extended family."

Eden liked the idea of having an extended family, and this particular one was growing on her by the hour. Could she really have this as her new reality?

Gabriel propped her up on his thigh to open the door to his suite, and then he stepped in sideways, kicked the door shut, and locked it. That sound made her flinch.

"Are you going to spank me?"

"What do you think?"

She sighed. "Will you tell me what happened at the diner first?"

"Yep." He sat on the couch and arranged her sideways on his lap.

"Was Marv mad?" she asked as she fiddled with the front of her shirt. Of course, Marv had been mad. Marv was always mad.

"Livid, especially when I came to the back room with three

of my brothers without announcing myself. The vein on his head bulged out."

Eden winced.

"Luckily, he hadn't even touched your purse. I don't think it had occurred to him it was there. It's in my saddle bag. We can grab it later."

"Was that it? You just found my purse and left?" she asked, hopeful.

Gabriel shook his head. "Not even close. Took me a while to impress upon that asshole that it would be in his best interest to reveal the names of the four men who'd harassed you."

Her eyes went wide. "Did you threaten him?"

"Definitely. But we're not gangsters, Eden. I wasn't going to break his knees or anything."

"Oh, good." She blew out a breath. That had been exactly what she'd been thinking. Had he read her mind?

He slid a hand up her back and rested his fingers on her neck. "He's not going to bother you, Little one. I promise. I even got your last paycheck."

She sat up straighter. "Oh, wow. And you didn't break his knees?"

He chuckled, his body jiggling and making her bounce on his lap. "I can be persuasive without breaking any bones, Little girl." He squeezed her neck.

"So, I can go back to my apartment now?"

He gave her a stern look. "Definitely not. Did you forget about the four men who harassed you?"

Right. "But you got their names, so maybe it's not so bad?"

"Ladybug, it's very bad. Those are not nice men, and they got your address from Marv. I'm sure they went straight there. I'd bet they're watching your apartment even now. I don't like the idea of taking you there even with ten men as backup."

Her shoulders fell. "What if they never stop harassing me?"

Her lip quivered at the possibility. "How will I be able to go home?"

"Eden, I need you to listen to Daddy."

She stared at him.

"You *are* home. This is your home now. You will always be safe here. I promise. I know that's difficult to grasp because it happened so fast, and I'll give you all the time you need to believe me, but you're my Little girl. This is where you'll live. I'll take you to your apartment to get some things, but you'll stay by my side at all times, and several of my brothers will be with us. Whatever you want to bring back here, we'll pack up and take with us. Whatever you don't need, we'll put in storage or sell."

She licked her lips. "What if you change your mind and decide you don't like me? Then I won't have a place to live."

He shook his head. "That's not going to happen, Ladybug."

"But you haven't even had sex with me," she blurted, realizing it sounded absurd, which made her flush. "I mean, maybe we won't be compatible in bed, or I won't be able to please you or—"

He clapped a hand over her mouth. "Eden, stop. That's not even a thing. I don't have to have sex with you to know fireworks will go off the first time I do. There's no hurry."

She couldn't let go of this line of thinking, so she lowered his hand and continued, "I'm not very good at it."

"Good at what, Ladybug? Sex?" His brows lifted.

"Yes."

"How the hell is that even a thing, Little one?"

She raised her voice. "I don't know. Ask the guys I've slept with. None of them were pleased."

CHAPTER
NINE

abriel stiffened, his eyes going wide as he tried to control his fury. Who the fuck would tell this precious Little girl they weren't pleased with her in bed? Jesus.

"Eden, I would rather not speak to anyone who's ever been in your bed, especially if they led you to believe you weren't a treasured gift. I might be inclined to break knees, and that's not usually my style."

She lowered her shoulders and her gaze. Her hands were shaking, which infuriated him further. Apparently, a lot of people had been mean to her in the past. It made no sense to him. She was a gem among all precious stones. Someone to be worshiped. Someone he intended to dote on for the rest of his life.

As much as he hated to ask more questions, he needed more information. "Ladybug," he began as calmly as possible, "how many men have you slept with?"

"Three," she whispered.

"When was this?"

"One after the senior prom, one guy I dated from high

school a year after we graduated, and one guy who took me out a few years after that."

Gabriel took a deep breath. He needed to remain calm. "Eden," he said softly, "those guys were jerks. They didn't know what to do to please a woman."

"I was the common denominator," she murmured.

He shook his head and lifted her face with a finger under her chin. "No. I won't have you talking like that. For one thing, let's eliminate the first and second guys entirely. They were boys. Eighteen and nineteen? They probably didn't even know what a vagina was, let alone a clitoris. I don't know how old the next guy was, but he was just an asshole. Drop anything they ever said from your memory."

She stared at him. "You can't order me to forget things, Gabriel." She shuddered as if the mere mention brought back bad memories.

He drew in a breath. She had a point. He was being high-handed. "Then we'll just replace those memories, and then you'll know."

"Then I'll know what?"

"How unbelievably sensual and attractive you are. How good it feels to have a decent man bring you to ecstasy. What liars those boys were. The list is long."

She tried to look away, but he didn't let her. Instead, he lowered his lips until they hovered a breath from hers.

"I'm going to kiss you, Eden. I've wanted to kiss you from the moment I met you. When I kiss you, you're going to think of nothing but me, and you're going to know in your heart that you're mine."

Her eyes went wider. He could feel her pulse racing under his fingertips at her neck.

He continued, "You're going to forget where you are and what your name is, but you will know whose lips are worshiping yours, and you'll never forget it."

Without hesitating, he closed the scant distance and

brought his mouth to hers. He didn't start small or lead in with tiny pecks against her lips. He consumed her the way he'd wanted to from the moment he'd first found her crying on the sidewalk.

It only took a few seconds for Eden to soften to him. She let her lips part. She grabbed his shoulders. She even tipped her head to one side when he licked the seam of her lips.

Damn, she was precious. He'd known this kiss would be amazing, but it was much better than he'd expected. He liked how quickly she grew bold, leaning into him, moaning against his mouth, gripping him with her fingertips.

This was it for him. His woman. His Little girl. His perfect match.

He kissed her until she was panting, and they were both in need of oxygen. When he let their mouths part, he didn't move back more than an inch. He found and held her gaze, loving the stunned look on her face, her glazed eyes, and the way she licked her lips.

She had twisted to face him more fully, bending one knee so that her shin rested against his cock now.

He slid his hands down to cup her bottom. "Do you doubt me now?"

She gave him a slow smile. "Not about kissing."

He eased his hands up to her waist and tickled her, causing her to twist and turn until she fell to her side next to him on the couch cushion, batting at his hands. *"Gabriel,"* she squealed.

He stopped tickling to drop his hands on either side of her where she now lay on her back. "Are you saying the rest of your body was unaffected by that kiss?"

She sobered and planted her palms on his chest. "No. My body liked it fine."

"Fine?" he teased. He had every intention of turning that fine into fireworks in the next ten minutes, but she hadn't realized that yet.

She shrugged but giggled at the same time.

He sat up, lifted her by the hips, and quickly turned her around so that she was lying across his lap on her tummy.

"What are you doing?" she asked, her voice high-pitched.

"You owe me a spanking. Two of them."

She squirmed, trying to turn over, but he kept one hand on the small of her back and one on the backs of her thighs. She wasn't strong enough for him. "Two of them?" she said, her voice thin and breathless.

"Yep. One for running in the building. You could've fallen and hit your head. It was the only rule I gave you. You couldn't have forgotten the only rule you had."

She sighed.

"You also need a good hard spanking for the tree-hiding stunt."

"But it wasn't even my idea, and-and-and we weren't hiding. We were just climbing a tree."

Damn, but she was delightful. "Now, you owe me three spankings."

She gasped and twisted her head around to look at him. "Why?"

"Lying. Rule number two. Little girls who tell lies get their bottoms swatted. You didn't need me to specifically spell out that rule to assume it would be on the list."

She dropped her weight over him, going limp as though realizing she wasn't going to get out of this.

"I'm certain the other Little girls knew they would get spanked when they raced outside to hide in the tree, and I'm equally sure they made that clear to you. Am I wrong?"

"No, Sir."

His breath hitched, and his cock doubled in size at the honorific. "I like that politeness, Ladybug. I'll like it even better when you call me Daddy." He slid his hand up to rub her bottom, enjoying the way she squirmed yet again.

"Is it going to hurt?" she asked softly.

"Yes, but you're going to enjoy it."

"That's silly."

"You'll see. You're going to *see* a lot of things in the next few minutes."

"What if I don't like it?"

"Then I'll find other ways to discipline you, and just to be clear, my spankings will hurt. Naughty Little girls need sore bottoms as a reminder to obey their Daddies."

"You're not making any sense, you know," she argued.

He chuckled. "Spread your legs, Ladybug." He patted the backs of her thighs.

"Why?"

"Eden…" he warned. "Do what Daddy says."

"Fine." She humphed as she parted her thighs about an inch.

"Wider, Ladybug."

Without argument, she obeyed him this time, and she also started panting.

"Good girl. Now, let me explain the types of spankings. When you do something unsafe like running through the compound, leaving without permission, climbing onto a chair to reach something, or touching knives in the kitchen, Daddy will spank you to reinforce the rule. Hard and fast."

She gasped but said nothing. Her thighs stiffened as he continued to rub them. She couldn't control her body's reactions to his words.

"There are other types of spankings, Little girl. One of them is the type you'll get when you and your friends conspire to do something naughty for the sole purpose of getting your bottoms swatted. Did you notice all the other girls plotted that tree adventure on purpose?"

"Yeah, but I still don't understand why," she murmured.

"You're curious, though."

She shrugged. So cute.

"There is one more type of spanking. The kind you'll get

when you need the release, and you come to me and ask me to spank you."

She arched her chest up, twisted her head again, and shot him a shocked look. "Now, you're just making this stuff up."

"Nope." He chuckled. "You'll see." He eased his hand up to the waistband of her leggings. "When I spank you, it will always be on your bare bottom so I can monitor how red your skin is getting. I never ever want to injure you. I will only swat you hard enough to sting and make you wince for the rest of the day when you sit down. Never hard enough for the effects to last into the next day."

Eden dropped her weight against him again. "Whatever..."

He smiled. She didn't believe a word of what he'd said, and it would be his pleasure to show her the truth. He was confident from all the squirming and little noises she was making that she would love having her pretty little bottom pinkened.

She said nothing as he eased both her leggings and her panties down to her knees. She took the opportunity to close her thighs as he removed her tennis shoes and set them on the floor.

Gabriel patted her creamy white skin. She was gorgeous from head to toe. He couldn't wait until she was ready for him to taste every inch of her. "Spread your knees again, Ladybug. Pull your panties and the elastic of your leggings tight."

She shuddered, but after hesitating, she did as he'd told her. She also set her forehead against her folded hands, panting. He was already affecting her, and he hadn't started yet. He was confident she was going to enjoy every moment of this spanking. He could smell her arousal. He was dying to reach between her thighs and touch her pussy to prove how wet she was, but she wasn't ready for that yet. She would be soon.

"I'm going to start gently, Ladybug, to warm up your bottom. Try not to stiffen. It will feel better if you relax your muscles."

She nodded subtly. That was enough.

Gabriel kept one hand on the small of her back to ensure she didn't squirm away as he lifted the other and gave her the first swat.

She gasped from nothing more than the shock. He hadn't struck her hard enough to even see the faint outline of his palm. He did it again and then four more times, alternating between butt cheeks.

Her skin was barely pink when he rubbed it. "Not so bad, right?"

She shook her head.

"That's just a warmup, Little one. Are you ready for more?"

CHAPTER
TEN

Eden couldn't wrap her head around what was happening here. She was lying across this giant man's lap, bottom exposed, legs spread, while he spanked her...?

If someone would have told her twenty-four hours ago she'd be in this position today, she would have laughed at them. She hadn't believed anyone would have wanted her in this position, or any position for that matter.

Gabriel had made it clear that he wanted her. He wanted to spank her, but he also wanted to dominate her and Daddy her. And he wanted to sleep with her...

His next swats were firmer, jolting her back to the present. The sting was an odd sensation. It wasn't bad. It made her feel alive in a way she hadn't felt in a long time.

Eden had been doing nothing but existing for a long time. Work, sleep, eat, repeat. She paid the rent and utilities. Sometimes, she got together with Carlee for lunch or coffee, but that was it. She didn't have any close friends, mostly because she couldn't afford to go out but also partly because she didn't care for the bar scene, and she certainly didn't want to put herself into a situation where people might make fun of her or belittle her or remind her how unattractive she was.

As the swats got harder, the burn grew, and she found herself craving more. It was oddly euphoric. She felt like she was floating out of her body, absorbing the slight pain and enjoying it.

When he stopped, his hand rubbing her bottom, she whimpered and arched her butt into his hand. She also squeezed her thighs together.

He chuckled. "Next time I tell you something, you'll believe me," he teased.

She dropped her forehead, panting, totally embarrassed. He was right. She liked this spanking.

"Spread your legs, Eden..." he warned.

Her whimper was louder, and she trembled as she obeyed him.

"Good girl." He set his palm on her thigh and eased it up until he was almost touching her sex. "I know you're wet and needy. Daddy will take care of that when I'm done. I won't let you squeeze your little clit tight while I spank you. You'll keep your thighs parted so your pussy feels exposed."

She shuddered at his words, the oddest sensation rushing through her body. Needy? That described her exactly, but she didn't know exactly what it meant. If she wasn't mistaken, she was about to orgasm, and she'd never experienced that before.

Was it possible? She'd never even tried to do it to herself, and Gabriel wasn't touching her. Not where it mattered.

But Lord knew she wanted him to.

He stroked her inner thigh gently, so close to her folds.

A mewl escaped her lips, embarrassing her further.

"Not yet, Ladybug. Daddy isn't done spanking you." His voice was deeper than usual. Gravelly. Was he enjoying this? Was he aroused from spanking her? Surely not. No one had gotten aroused from doing anything to her, and certainly not from seeing her naked.

Eden pulled her arms in close to her chest, trying to control the multitude of sensations rushing through her and threatening to send her spiraling out of control.

Suddenly, he was spanking her again, but this time it felt different. More intense. It hurt more but in a good way. She craved it. She wanted more. Harder. Faster. She wanted him to punish her, and not just for running or hiding, but for all the negative thoughts in her head. He seemed to be chasing them away. Was that a thing?

The last few swats were at the juncture of her bottom and her thighs, and she gasped as he finished rubbing that spot. She realized she was arching her bottom up high, and her toes were curled under, holding her up.

She was panting. She was also stiffening to keep from shaking.

Gabriel's other hand was on the small of her back, and he reached under her T-shirt, pushing it up so he could touch the bare skin of her lower belly. "I love the way you purr when you're aroused, Ladybug," he whispered as his spanking hand slid up her inner thigh again.

Her face heated. Was she purring?

His hand moved slowly, too slowly, teasing her sensitive skin. When his fingertips got within a millimeter of her needy sex, he pressed down, tugging on the skin, causing her lower lips to part. Air hit the wetness, and she lifted her head and moaned.

"What do you need, Ladybug?"

She dug her toes deeper into the cushion. He wanted her to talk?

"Tell Daddy what you need, Eden," he encouraged.

She licked her lips, desperate enough to ask. "Touch me. Please, Daddy." That word slid off her tongue so easily. She'd never felt Littler than she did at this moment, stretched out over his lap, submitting to his discipline, her bottom red hot from being spanked like a naughty Little girl.

She wouldn't let herself believe he could really want her forever, but she liked how he made her feel and the sound of the honorific. *Daddy...*

"Oh, Ladybug. That pleases me. You deserve a reward." He stopped tormenting her, bringing his fingers to her labia. For a moment, he stroked over the swollen, greedy folds, and then he parted them and dragged a finger through the center. "So wet for me."

She stopped breathing as she arched farther, rising onto her hands and knees, straddling his thighs. She was completely out of control. Her body was spinning again. If he let go of her, she would spin off his lap and fly away.

Gabriel pushed her T-shirt higher, exposing her breasts so that they swayed. They felt heavy. Swollen. Her nipples were hard points that wanted to be touched. What was happening to her?

Gabriel tapped her clit, and she cried out. "Please, Daddy..." She wasn't even positive about what she needed or wanted, but she knew it was something, and she knew he would give it to her.

"I've got you, Ladybug." His palm on her back steadied her. His hand between her legs stroked over her folds again before flicking her clit rapidly.

Something was building inside her, growing and tightening and threatening to erupt, and suddenly, it all flew apart. She screamed as she crested some strange precipice. Her body shook violently as her clit pulsed against his fingers.

Waves of pleasure consumed her as she floated out of her body. Bliss. Total bliss.

Just as she was about to collapse over his lap, Gabriel lifted her into his arms and gently turned her over so he was cradling her. He pulled her tightly against his chest, his hands around her, keeping her from flying away.

He kissed her temple. "You are the most precious Little girl ever, Eden. Never forget it."

She wasn't able to control the shaking, and he pulled a throw blanket over her partially nude body, tucking it around her.

She rolled into him, burrowing her face in his chest. She'd never been this close to another human being or felt this cherished.

He stroked her back over the blanket. "Was that your first orgasm, Ladybug?"

She stiffened, embarrassed, but slowly nodded.

He held her even tighter. "I'm a very lucky man."

Was he? Right about now, she was thinking she was a very lucky woman. If she never experienced something like that again in her life, at least she would have the memory of this encounter. Maybe it had been a coincidence, an accident. Maybe she couldn't do it again.

"You're mine, Little girl." He kissed her forehead and continued kissing her all over, leaning her back to kiss her cheeks, nose, and lips.

She moaned into his mouth as he deepened the kiss, letting her tongue tangle with his as they seemed to merge.

His broad palm, fingers splayed against her back, held her up. Her bottom was tingly and hot from the spanking. It was also exposed. Her leggings and panties were tangled around her shins.

When he broke the kiss, he kept her face close, staring into her eyes, keeping her connected, rocking her. "Mine, Ladybug. Mine."

Her breathing quickened. He was so intense. Determined. Certain. She wished she could be as sure about anything as he was.

Eventually, he rose from the couch, still cradling her. He carried her to the bedroom and lowered her onto the bed, carefully rolling her to her stomach.

She whimpered at the exposure when he removed the blanket. She scrambled to reach down for her panties.

He stilled her with a palm to the small of her back. "Stay, Little one. Let me examine your bottom so I can make sure I didn't strike you too hard."

She held her breath while he leaned over her, holding her down with one hand while he poked around her bottom with the other. It should have been humiliating. Her cheeks were certainly heated again. But instead, she felt cared for in a way she couldn't remember ever experiencing.

"Don't move, Ladybug. I'm going to put some cream on your skin to lessen the sting." He released her to open the drawer on the bedside table, and she turned her head to the side to watch him open a tube of ointment and squeeze some onto his fingers. She held her breath as he rubbed it into her burning skin.

"How does it feel, Ladybug?"

"Fine."

He chuckled. "I'm going to need more words than that." He put the cream away, lifted her off the bed, stood her on her feet, and carefully pulled her panties over her bottom before following with her leggings. When he was done, he righted her shirt, held her hips, and met her gaze as he sat on the edge of the bed. "I know you enjoyed it." He winked. "But was it too hard or too soft?"

She pursed her lips and shrugged. How could she possibly know?

"Don't let it embarrass you, Ladybug. Most Little girls like to get spanked. I told you that was the case. That's why the other girls conspired to hide in the tree. They pull naughty shenanigans like that every few days. Now you know why." He smiled and kissed her nose.

"Seems kind of silly."

Gabriel chuckled. "It's a pretty common aspect among people who enjoy age play."

"Oh." Her head was still reeling from the intense orgasm. Her legs were trembling and threatening to give out on her.

Gabriel must have noticed because he swept her off her feet and settled her on his lap. "You're a very responsive Little girl, Eden. Why haven't you explored your sensual side before?"

She looked down and fiddled with her hands in her lap. He wanted to talk about sex? And, more specifically, masturbation? She didn't think she could do that.

He rubbed her back. "I can understand why none of the boys you had sex with when you were younger were knowledgeable enough to take care of your needs, too. I don't like it, but it's not uncommon. They were selfish and only cared about themselves. But did you try touching yourself, Ladybug?"

She shook her head.

"Why not?" He stroked under her chin with a finger but didn't force her to look at him. "Did someone tell you it was wrong, Little one?"

She shook her head again.

"Tell Daddy what you're thinking."

"I just didn't know," she murmured.

"Ah. You didn't realize what it would be like."

She shook her head, wishing he would stop asking questions about this topic.

He cupped her face and kissed her forehead. "I know you're embarrassed, but I don't want you to be. Not with me. Not when it's just the two of us. I want to know everything about you. I want to know what you like and don't like, what you've done and not done. I'm going to ask you a million questions so that I can make sure your legs are wobbly every time I make you come." His voice was teasing at the end.

She whimpered and leaned her forehead against his chest to hide.

He chuckled. "You're so precious, Little one. I'm debating what we should do next. Hmmm."

She finally lifted her head. "You said we could go to my apartment."

"Yep. We will. I'm trying to decide if I should strip your

clothes off first so I can spread you out on the bed and eat your pussy until you scream so loud they can hear you in the bike shop."

She gasped. Had he really just said that?

His grin made her clench her thighs together. "It's the only way I'll be able to prove to you that what just happened wasn't a one-time thing. You can and will be able to reach that level of ecstasy many times, Little one." He tapped his lips as if deliberating.

She shook her head and tried to scramble off his lap.

He didn't let her go, though. He kept a hand firmly around her hips. "I don't want you to spend the rest of the morning thinking you can't do that again, Ladybug."

She shoved at his chest, beyond embarrassed. "Daddy…" She immediately pursed her lips, shocked that she'd called him *Daddy* yet again.

He laughed. "Okay. Okay. Calm down. But just so you know, this shy, easily embarrassed side of you is precious beyond words. It's impossible not to tease you. We can go to your apartment, but after lunch, you're going to take a nap, and after your nap, I'm going to thrust my tongue into your pussy until you come so hard you believe me. Think about that while we're packing your things."

This time when she shoved at him, he lifted her off his lap and set her on her feet. He didn't let go, though. "Look at Daddy."

She shook her head and looked anywhere but at his face.

"We're not leaving until you look Daddy in the eyes, Ladybug," he admonished. He didn't let go of her, and he was strong.

She finally drew in a breath and looked at him.

"Good girl. You are adorable. I'm so damn happy I want to shout it to anyone who will listen. But on a serious note, I need you to obey me while we're outside the compound. I'm serious about this. What I say goes. It's for your safety. Understood?"

"Yes, Sir," she murmured. He was serious. This was important to him. He was really concerned for her safety.

"Good girl. When Daddy tells you to do something safety-related, I expect you to obey immediately. If you don't, I will blister your little bottom harder than what you just experienced, and it won't be followed by an orgasm. It will be followed by you standing in the corner with your pants around your knees, holding your shirt up so your naughty red bottom is on display during your timeout. Do you understand?"

She nodded.

"Words, Little one."

"Yes, Sir."

"Yes, Sir, what?"

"Yes, I'll obey you when it's safety-related," she murmured. She was trembling because this was so intense. He was extremely serious. Once again, she felt like he cared. He cared so much that he might boss her around to ensure she was safe.

She could be miffed by how highhanded he was, but she felt warm and tingly instead. She liked feeling like someone cared about her enough to keep her safe. Could she really be his?

CHAPTER
ELEVEN

Gabriel didn't like it. He didn't like taking his Little girl to her apartment. He would have preferred leaving her at the compound. He had a bad feeling that wouldn't go away. Even though Steele, Talon, and Kade were following him on their bikes, he worried.

Maybe this was what happened when one became a Daddy. They worried. He knew all three of those men worried, not just about their own Littles but each other's. He did, too. He always kept an eye on all the women in the compound. It was nothing compared to how he felt now about Eden, though.

The Little girl had burrowed her way into his heart and was there to stay. He cringed at the idea of her getting so much as a scratch or a booboo. He would panic like an overprotective Daddy. Which he was. Apparently, it was a club. *Welcome. The membership is free, but the angst is real.*

Gabriel had brought his SUV so they could fill it with boxes of her belongings. Eden was sitting in the passenger seat next to him, but she hadn't said a word since they'd left the compound. Her arms were crossed, and she was still miffed that he'd wanted her to sit in the back. Not just in the back but in the center.

Gabriel knew the rear center was the safest spot in the SUV. If any asshole ran a light or a stop sign and hit them from any angle, the safest place in the car would be the center back row.

Eden had put up a fuss, including stomping her foot when he'd opened the rear seat. It had been difficult for him to keep a straight face as he'd watched her have her first tantrum. She had no idea how adorable she was, even when she was mad.

He hadn't been kidding, but when he'd caught the other Daddies chuckling, he'd finally relented and let her sit up front. He'd lifted her into the SUV, though, and then he'd buckled her seatbelt and tugged it tight.

She'd glared at him, crossed her arms, and was still sitting like that now. Likely, she was still nursing her previous mad from the argument they'd had before they'd left his suite. That argument had begun when she'd insisted she needed more adult clothes to leave the compound. After all, he'd told her previously that she could wear adult clothes when she was out in the real world.

Gabriel's defense had been that they wouldn't see a single soul. They were going straight to her apartment and back. The clothes she'd worn last night were still dirty in the hamper. Obviously, she hadn't had anything else to wear in his suite.

In the end, he'd given her two options: stay at the compound under the supervision of some of his other brothers or wear what she was wearing and get in the SUV. He'd even counted to three.

His Little girl had stomped out the door all the way to the car, where she'd moved from one tantrum to the next. Gabriel still had trouble controlling his grin, and he needed to because she would be fuming angry if she thought he was laughing at her.

He was assuredly not laughing *at* her. He was simply so

damn happy to have found her and beyond pleased with her spunky side that indicated she was going to be a handful. *His* handful. He'd much rather have a Little girl who argued with him and kept him on his toes than one who meekly accepted everything he said without question. That would get boring in a hurry.

Except when it came to safety. Hopefully, he'd impressed that on her firmly enough. He'd tried to pull the safety card with regard to strapping her in behind him, but admittedly, that had been feeble at best.

"Wait for Daddy to come around and help you out, Ladybug," he said as he parked and turned off the engine.

She shot him a glare. "I'm not a baby, Gabriel."

He sighed as he exited the car and rounded to her side, where he, of course, found her standing on the ground, leaning casually against the door as though she'd been waiting for him for an hour. The little stinker even looked at her nails from the fake boredom.

He crowded her against the car, tipped her chin back, and met her gaze. "Do you think if you defy me enough times, I'll grow tired of you and dump you?"

She swallowed. "Yes."

He had been afraid that might be the case. The only thing he could do to reassure her he was never going anywhere was to exercise patience. He closed the distance and set a kiss on her lips. "It won't happen, Ladybug. You can be as obstinate as you want for ten years, and I'll still be here flexing my fingers in an effort to avoid carpel tunnel from spanking you so often."

She gasped. "Can we go inside now, *Daddy*?" She said that last word with a tremendous amount of snark.

Gabriel knew exactly what was happening. Eden had had bad experiences in her life. People had made fun of her and had not been kind. The three men she'd had short relationships with had done nothing to help her self-esteem. She didn't trust Gabriel to stay with her.

He needed to be patient and understanding and prove her wrong. He would succeed. He cupped her face and brought his very close. "Yes, Ladybug. Remember what I said about obeying me while we're here." He lifted a brow.

She sighed dramatically and rolled her eyes. "Yes, Daddy." More snark and sass.

Ignoring it, he kissed her. He would address her behavior later, after they packed up her stuff, after he fed her lunch, and after he made her come with his face buried between her legs...

Steele, Talon, and Kade had come on their bikes, and when Gabriel turned around, he found them waiting patiently on the curb.

Gabriel took Eden's hand. "What's your apartment number, Little one?"

"Five twenty-three."

"Let's go." He threaded his fingers with her smaller ones to keep her from tugging free of his grip. He also remembered to slow his gate so she wouldn't have to jog to keep up with him.

The apartment building was large. Six floors. Her unit was on the fifth. It wasn't in the best part of town. It was low-income housing. The lobby was relatively clean but in need of paint and updates. Gabriel assumed the inside of her apartment would be similar.

They rode to the fifth floor in silence, and when they stepped out, she said, "Mine's the last one on the right."

Kade led the way. Gabriel pulled her keys out of his pocket and released her hand, only long enough to unlock the door. The moment he pushed it open, he winced and stepped back, pulling her with him. "Fuck," he muttered.

He didn't know why he was surprised to see her place ransacked. That was exactly what he'd feared. The Devil's

Jesters were not good people. They'd been furious with her, and Marv had admitted to giving them her address. Why would he be shocked to find out they'd come straight here?

"I've got her," Talon said as he gently pulled Eden away from the door.

"Thank you," Gabriel muttered as he entered with Steele and Kade.

"Jesus..." Kade murmured. "The Jesters don't fuck around, do they?"

"Apparently not." Steele had his phone out and was already tapping away at the screen. "I know the president. I'll arrange a meeting."

Gabriel glanced at him. "Slash? That guy's an asshole. How is a meeting going to help?"

Steele rubbed his forehead. "If he doesn't meet with us and address this issue, the repercussions will be tremendous."

That was the truth. Gabriel wasn't usually prone to violence, but he was feeling pretty violent right now. Maybe breaking a few kneecaps wasn't a bad idea. As the chaplain for the MC, he was usually the voice of reason—the guy people went to for advice. Not a man who condoned violence. But no one had ever come after his own Little girl before. His blood was boiling.

Gabriel and Kade searched the place, looking in every closet and behind every door, including under the bed. When he leaned into the bathroom, his breath hitched, and he hesitated. "Fuck," he muttered.

"What is it?" Kade asked from behind him.

Gabriel pointed at the mirror above the sink as Kade leaned through the doorway next to him.

Your cunt is mine, bitch.

"Jesus," Kade whispered.

"Keep Eden out of here," Gabriel growled.

"Definitely. Whoever it is, they aren't here now," Kade said.

Gabriel shuffled back toward the door to the apartment, where he found Eden sniffling in Talon's arms. "Is it bad?" she asked in barely a whisper.

"Yes, Ladybug. It's pretty bad. I'm not going to sugarcoat it. Would you rather I take you back to the compound and then clean up this mess?"

She shook her head. "No. I want to get some of my things."

"Okay." He took her hand and led her into the apartment. He hadn't been kidding. The place had been flipped. Every single piece of furniture was upside down. Every drawer had been emptied onto the floor. Whoever had come in here had even taken a knife to her bed and stabbed the mattress so many times that the bedroom was filled with fluff.

Eden gasped as silent tears rolled down her face. She yanked her hand free of Gabriel's and wandered around, picking up things and righting them as if standing up a lamp or setting a plate on the counter would make a difference.

When she turned toward Gabriel, she said, "I keep replaying last night in my head, wondering if I could've handled things differently. I snapped when that guy pinched my ass. What if I hadn't thrown the soda in his face? What if I'd laughed them off when they'd taunted me?"

Gabriel glanced over his shoulder to make sure no one else was listening. They had all made themselves scarce. They were in her bedroom. "And told them the color of your fucking pubic hair?" Gabriel hissed. He shook his head. "No, Ladybug. They were way the fuck out of line. You did nothing wrong."

She swiped at tears, nearly breaking his heart. He didn't like to see his Little girl so upset. Shoulders slumping, she passed him and headed for her bedroom.

Gabriel followed her to find the other men making piles of clothes and tucking stuffing from the mattress back into one of the slashes, probably to get it out of the way so they could see.

Eden gasped as she ran across the room. She grabbed something off the floor, pulled it to her chest, and sank to her knees. Sobs filled the room.

Gabriel rushed toward her, pushing things out of the way to get to his girl. He dropped onto his knees behind her and wrapped his arms around her. He couldn't see what she was holding, but it was obviously important to her.

He held her and rocked gently while she cried, waiting for her to slow to sniffles before saying, "Can Daddy see?"

Her hands were shaking as she lowered them from her chest to reveal a stuffed ladybug. His head had been almost severed from his body. It was hanging on by a thread.

Gabriel's heart hurt, and rage filled him at the same time. He fought to control that last emotion. "What's his name?"

"Spot," she sobbed. "Why would someone do this?"

"Because some people have so much ugliness inside them that all they know how to do is hurt others." Gabriel cradled the stuffie's head. "You know what? The cut was clean right at his neck. I'm certain it can be sewn back on, and you will hardly notice."

"Do you think so?" she asked, tipping her head back to look at him with the saddest eyes.

"Yep. Let's find a box to put him in."

"I think Carlee knows how to sew," she said.

"I think you're right. I've seen her stitching a few things in the clubhouse. I bet she can fix Spot right up." It was going to take a lot more than a needle and thread to fix the pain Gabriel was feeling. It was going to take a lengthy trip to the punching bag hanging in the gym at the compound before he would be calm enough to keep from breaking knees.

Gabriel planted his feet on the floor, scooped Eden into his arms, and lifted her as she hugged Spot against her chest, cradling his head. She kissed the stuffie over and over. "I'm sorry, Spot. I promise someone will fix you."

Damn, she was precious.

Finally, she lifted her gaze and wiggled to get down. "I should pack."

He lowered her to her feet just as Kade stepped forward, holding a shoe box. "How about we put Spot in here? I'll make sure he gets into one of the boxes we're taking to the clubhouse."

"Thank you," Eden murmured. She relinquished Spot, rubbed her eyes, and stood taller. After a deep breath, she started grabbing clothes and helping the others put things in boxes.

"What about these plants?" Steele asked from near the window.

Eden spun around and gasped yet again. She ran over to look at the mess of dirt and leaves. Once again, she dropped to her knees. "No. No-no-no-no-no." Her hand trembled as she reached out to slide her palm gently under the largest plant.

Gabriel was seeing red. Those fucking Jesters had messed with the wrong woman. If he didn't control himself, he was going to end up in jail.

Steele squatted beside her. "I think the plant is fine, Little one. The dirt is still packed around it. The stems aren't even broken. Just the flowerpot."

"I've got an idea. Don't move," Talon said before hurrying from the room. He returned a minute later holding a blender. He grabbed a pile of fluff from the floor, stuffed it in the bottom over the blades, and then knelt beside Eden. As carefully as possible, he lifted the plant and eased the entire thing down into the top of the blender. "Perfect. The pot was almost this exact size. I bet we have some pots hanging around the clubhouse that need a plant."

Eden stared at him with tears running down her cheeks. "Thank you," she managed to whisper. "That was my father's plant. I took it with me from his house after he died. All it ever needs is a little water. Do you think it will survive?"

"I do, Little one. I really do." Talon grinned at her.

Gabriel couldn't move or breathe. He was so grateful for these men he called his brothers. Each and every one of them. They were being so fucking kind to his Little girl. They hardly knew her, and they treated her like one of their own. He was truly blessed.

CHAPTER
TWELVE

E den was exhausted three hours later when her Daddy guided her to his suite. She didn't even argue about taking a nap. She wanted nothing more than to curl up under the covers in his bed and fall asleep.

Gabriel pulled the covers back, sat her on the mattress, and removed her shoes. After helping her lay back, he pulled her leggings off, too, before shifting her to the middle of the bed and pulling the covers over her.

He was the best man in the world, and even after everything that had happened today, he was still being so kind to her. He hadn't flinched when she'd been argumentative earlier. He hadn't hesitated for a second when he'd found her apartment ransacked. He could have just thrown up his hands, declared the place not worth it, and taken her back to the clubhouse. Instead, he'd pushed up his sleeves and started sorting through things.

All the men had worked for over an hour, making piles and packing boxes. With five of them, they made quick work. They were so kind, asking her about every little thing to make sure it wasn't important before discarding it in one of the giant trash bags.

Gabriel tucked Coco in her arms and leaned over to kiss her temple. "Rest, Ladybug. You'll feel better after a nap."

"Are you going to spank me for being naughty this morning?"

He shook his head. "No, Little one. You don't need another spanking today. You've had a very tough day. You need rest and snuggles."

"But I was bad, and I argued about safety." She stared up at him. She shocked even herself with her odd request.

Gabriel sat on the edge of the mattress and rubbed her hip. "Me asking you to sit in the backseat is admittedly a bit over the top as far as safety is concerned. The chances of a cement truck slamming into the passenger side of my SUV are pretty damn slim." He gave her a small smile. "I would like you to let Daddy help you in and out of cars, but that's because I like to do things for you. It's not as though you ran out into traffic. You stayed right next to the car after you got out."

She pursed her lips, not commenting.

He smiled broader. "I bet you're thinking a good spanking would help purge some of the stressful, icky feelings from dealing with your apartment."

He understands. She released her lips and nodded.

"That's not unreasonable, Ladybug, but I don't want to spank you so soon after I did this morning. How about if, while you nap, I think of another way to help you relax, okay?"

She nodded. "Okay, Daddy." It was getting easier to call him that. It was getting easier to trust him, too.

"Good girl." He kissed her forehead and rose. "Sleep. I'll be in the living room if you need me."

When he turned back to face her from the doorway, she said, "Daddy?"

"Yes, Ladybug?"

"I know you're really, really angry with those men. Please don't plot ways to break their knees, okay? I need you."

His smile was genuine and warmed her heart. "I won't, Ladybug. You have my word."

She hugged Coco tightly as he left the room. He'd closed the blinds, dimming the room slightly. When she inhaled deeply, she drew in his scent from the pillow, and it made her smile. She'd only met him last night, and already she knew his scent and loved it.

Gabriel had been a rock today. He'd held her together time and again when she'd started crying. She'd been argumentative before they'd gone to her apartment for no good reason except to see if she could push him away. He'd called her on that and insisted she could not. Was he for real?

She hugged Coco close, unable to stop smiling even though her life was a shambles by all accounts. Well, most accounts. She'd definitely lost her job, and there was no chance she could go back to her apartment. She'd never feel safe there again.

On the flip side, she'd met a wonderful man who was unwavering in his insistence she was his. He'd given her an orgasm. The memory made her squirm, and she closed her eyes tightly as she recalled how good it had felt to have his fingers on her—down there. Could he really do it again? He'd told her he would. In fact, he'd told her he would do it with his mouth.

She squeezed her thighs together. His mouth? Wasn't that kind of gross? She wasn't born yesterday. She was twenty-six years old. She knew people had oral sex; she just hadn't ever entertained the idea that she'd be one of them or even that she'd find someone she wanted to have sex with ever again.

The idea of having sex with Gabriel freaked her out a bit. What if it ended up being like all the other times she'd had sex? Boring, quick, and uneventful, with the addition that all three previous partners had acted like her lack of interest was her fault and she was weird.

Had it actually been *their* fault? She certainly hadn't had any trouble getting aroused when Gabriel had touched her.

She squirmed, rubbing her legs together. Her heart rate picked up at the thought of Daddy touching her. With her eyes closed, she could picture him rubbing her sore bottom and then stroking through her folds. Somehow, those two things had been connected—the spanking and the orgasm.

Her bottom was still hot now, and she lowered one hand behind her to rub it before easing that hand around to the front and cupping her sex. When she let her fingers graze over her folds through the panties, her breath hitched.

Holy shit. She'd been missing out. At twenty-six years old, she'd never masturbated. She'd never considered touching herself. She hadn't really thought she was a sexual person, especially after the experiences she'd had with all three men she'd been with.

She stroked over her clit next, and her eyes rolled back. Her mouth fell open, and she couldn't resist reaching into her panties to touch her clit directly. Why had she never done this before?

She found the little nub swollen and wet. Her panties were soaked. The nerve endings in that tiny part of her body seemed to be on fire. When she circled her clit, it grew larger. When she pinched it, a whimper escaped, or maybe it was more like a moan.

"Ladybug." The nickname Daddy had given her resonated through the room as a harsh command, and she gasped as her eyes shot open, her gaze jerking to the door. He wasn't there, though. It was still open just a few inches.

Her heart beat so fast her ears were ringing. Had he heard her moan from the living room? She froze with her hand still in her panties, mortification consuming her.

Suddenly, he opened the door and leaned into the room. He opened his mouth and then closed it. She'd never seen him doubtful, but he was right now. Finally, he swallowed and spoke. "Ladybug…" he began in a much softer voice, "I hesitate to order you not to touch yourself. After this morning, I suspect you're more curious than ever. You're a grown woman who deserves to take the time to find out what you like and don't like. I want you to know your body. On the flip side, I also want to own your orgasms. It's a conundrum."

She didn't dare breathe or move. Did he know her hand was inside her panties? Probably.

He drew in a deep breath. "Right now, you need to nap, naughty girl. If you do that, I'll let you come after you wake up. I really want to swallow your second orgasm."

She gasped, eyes wide. "Swallow it?"

He chuckled. "Yep. I want my mouth on your sweet pussy when you come."

He had mentioned that before. It was still startling to her. Her fingers were still on her clit, and when she tapped it, she nearly detonated. She felt mischievous. Her breath hitched again. She was pretty sure her body shook with tremors.

"Ladybug… Show me your hands."

She might have been emotionally exhausted from the day's events, and she might have been sorrowful for her naughty behaviors earlier, but she was feeling defiant and sassy. She shook her head.

Gabriel's brows went up. "Are you openly defying your Daddy?"

She nodded slowly and touched her clit again, loving the naughty feeling that accompanied the growing need. They went together. They went with the spanking he'd given her earlier. She was well aware of the slight burn in the skin of her derriere.

Daddy stepped farther into the room, sauntering toward her. He didn't stop until he stood at the side of the bed, and then he slowly tugged on the covers until they were completely off her body, exposing her and the fact that her hand was definitely still down her panties, cupping her sex.

Boldly, she stroked her clit again, and in a whiny voice, she said, "I can't sleep, Daddy. I need this first."

He reached for her bare legs, tugged them so that she swung around sideways on the bed on her back, and then grabbed her panties and hauled them off her body.

She gasped as he lifted her hand from her sex and brought it to his mouth. He sucked her fingers into his mouth and held them there while he removed her socks, his gaze never leaving hers.

After he released her fingers with a small pop, he pushed her shirt off over her head and tossed it on the floor. He hadn't spoken yet as he parted her thighs, wrapped his palms around them to spread them wider, and slowly inhaled with his face near her sex. "Mmm."

She flushed deeply. Was he smelling her? How embarrassing.

"My Little girl is very naughty."

She nodded.

"Do you think you can nap *after* I suck your pussy, Ladybug?"

She shrugged. She couldn't predict how she might feel afterward, but she wanted to find out.

"Let's see if I can wear you out." His face dropped so fast that she didn't have a single moment to wrap her head around his plan before his lips were on her. He dragged his tongue through her slit and flicked it over her clit.

Eden cried out, her hands going to his head, threading into the curls that had escaped the leather tie holding them back.

His soft beard rubbed against her tender skin as he sucked her clit.

She arched her back, lifting her stomach off the bed, but Gabriel tossed one forearm over her hips and held her down. He moaned and feasted on her sex as if this was a perfectly normal afternoon activity.

"Daddy..." she whimpered as her need grew. She was

going to come. It was building. The knot in her tummy was tight and ready to explode. It was just like last time but more intense. She wasn't as startled this time. She had some idea of what was coming.

He moaned against her sex as if he were eating the most delicious feast. With one hand on her inner thigh and one holding her hips down, he had her trapped, forced to accept what he was doing—and what he was doing was unraveling everything she'd ever believed about sex and orgasms.

Orgasms were a silly figment of everyone's imagination. Sex was a boring activity that benefited only the guy.

Until now. Until Gabriel. Until she'd met a Daddy who intended to prove her wrong.

He thrust his tongue into her just like he'd promised more than once today. God, it felt so good. Her body trembled from the need to come. She had a tight grip on his hair. A second later, his lips were on her clit again, and he sucked.

Eden's breath hitched, and she gasped as she hovered at the top of the mountain for two seconds, and then she was falling. Falling, falling, falling... Her entire body seemed to clench as her clit pulsed against his lips.

A strange sound filled the room, and she realized it was her. It was coming from her mouth. A deep moan. The sound of satisfaction.

She melted into the bed as her Daddy rained kisses all over her swollen labia. She was aware of a grin on her face, but she couldn't stop it. She was also splayed out wide, exposed. She didn't care about that either. At some point, she'd let go of his head because her hands were lying alongside her head by her ears. She was breathing heavily. She'd never felt so sated in her life.

Gabriel grabbed her hips and kissed a path to her breasts. When he flicked his tongue over one, she whimpered and arched her chest upward. How did she still have the energy?

He was smiling when he lifted his face and met her gaze.

"You are such a delightful gift, Ladybug. I'm the luckiest Daddy on earth. Do you feel better?"

She nodded, still grinning.

"Good. Do you think you can keep your fingers away from your pussy and take a nap like a good girl?"

She nodded again. She was finally tired.

He kissed her other nipple and tongued it, making her moan. "Insatiable little thing." He was still grinning as he leaned farther over her and kissed her lips.

She could taste herself on his mouth, but it didn't bother her. She was too pleased to care about something so naughty.

Like she was a delicate flower, Gabriel turned her so she was in the middle of the bed. He fluffed the pillow and tucked it under her head. He handed her Coco, pulled the covers over her, and kissed her again. "Sleep, Ladybug."

She closed her eyes. She was pretty sure she was still smiling as she fell asleep.

CHAPTER
THIRTEEN

Gabriel ran a hand through his hair as he paced around the conference room where he was meeting with several of his brothers. He didn't want to spend too much time outside of his suite. He hated the thought of Eden waking up to find him missing, but this was important. He needed to know what Steele had heard from the Devil's Jesters.

Besides, Gabriel had a baby monitor. He had his tablet open on the corner of the table so he could see if his Little girl moved even an inch. So far, she had not. She'd been exhausted and was out cold.

He didn't care that everyone in the room knew he was keeping an eye on his Little girl. Everyone in this room who also had a Little girl did the same thing on occasion. They understood the intense feelings he was experiencing. He finally did, too.

"Anyway, I spoke with Slash," Steele said.

Bear groaned. "That guy's a piece of work. His club is out of control. If he doesn't rein them in, there's going to be hell to pay."

Gabriel agreed. Lately, the Devil's Jesters had been hanging around Shadowridge far too often for his liking. They were known for wreaking havoc everywhere they went. There had been noise complaints from them revving their engines at all hours of the day and night. "Doesn't sound to me like Slash has any kind of grip on his members."

"That may be," Steele agreed, "but he's the president, so we need to go through him, and believe it or not, he agreed to a meeting."

"When?" Atlas asked, tapping his pen on the conference table. "And where?"

"Parking lot of the abandoned motel on the edge of town. Five o'clock."

Gabriel lifted a brow. "Sounds dangerous. How do we know they won't come in, guns blazing?"

"We don't," Steele agreed, "but I chose the location. I don't think the townsfolk will feel safe if over a dozen bikes come barreling through town, so we can't meet in a public location. It would scare the hell out of people."

"A dozen?" King asked. King was a firefighter, and he'd just gotten off a three-day shift at the firehouse. It was the same station where Doc worked as a medic.

Steele nodded. "Six of them. Six of us. No weapons allowed. Just a meeting."

Gabriel sighed as he thought about the possible ramifications. There was no way to avoid this meeting. If they didn't confront the Jesters and tell them to stand the fuck down when it came to Eden, she'd never be safe enough to leave the compound.

"You good with this, Gabriel?" Steele asked.

Gabriel nodded. It was necessary.

"You got people covering you at work today?" Bear asked.

"Yeah." Gabriel ran a hand through his hair. He did need to check in with the director and bring him up to speed on the changes in Gabriel's life. Bensen would understand. Gabriel was usually a workaholic, so no one would fault him for taking some time for himself for once.

Steele stood. "Good. We leave in an hour. Let's meet at the bikes." Steele pointed around the room. "Besides me and Gabriel, I'd like to have King, Doc, Talon, and Bear on this ride. That work for everyone?"

Heads nodded. Gabriel grabbed his tablet and headed back to his suite. Good men would have his back. He needed to spend the next hour with his girl.

Eden was just waking up as he slid into the bedroom. She rolled onto her back and then winced as she lifted her butt off the mattress. "Owie."

Even under the covers, he knew she was reacting to the sting from his earlier spanking. It shouldn't be bothering her that much by now, though. He frowned as he sat on the edge of the bed. "Let Daddy look at your bottom, Ladybug."

She shook her head as her cheeks turned pink. Her embarrassment was adorable. Would she always get so easily embarrassed? "It doesn't hurt, Daddy."

He narrowed his gaze. "Eden... What did I say about lying to Daddy?"

She giggled. The Little imp. And then she rolled slightly to one side, reached under the covers, and pulled out her bear. She held it up and pointed at his nose. "I must have let go of him while I was sleeping, and he crawled down to my butt, and then I rolled over him. His nose is hard."

Gabriel laughed so hard his body shook. "He crawled down there, did he?"

"Obviously." Her eyes were wide.

Gabriel dropped his hands on either side of her head and kissed her. "You are so fucking adorable."

"Is that a good thing?"

"It's a great thing. Are you ready to get up? I want to talk to you for a bit, then I have to head out with some of the guys for a while."

"Where are you going?"

He wouldn't lie to her. "To meet with some of the Devil's Jesters."

"About me…" she murmured.

"Yes."

"I don't want to cause a problem."

"Ladybug, you didn't cause the problem. Those bad men did when they harassed you at the diner. They multiplied that problem tenfold when they broke into your apartment and flipped it upside down. We have to put a stop to whatever they're planning."

She nodded.

Gabriel pulled the covers back and reached to lift her into his arms.

"Can I have my clothes back now, Daddy?"

He smiled as he rubbed her back. "Mmm. I kind of like you like this. Warm and soft and so very sexy."

Her flush deepened, and she looked away.

He lifted her chin. "I'm going to tell you that over and over until you believe it." He angled his hips forward against her thigh. "Feel that, Ladybug?"

She swallowed hard.

"Yep. That's what happens to my cock every time I'm near you. When you're naked, it's even more pronounced. So, don't doubt Daddy when I tell you you're smoking hot and the sexiest woman I've ever set eyes on." He narrowed his gaze at her.

"Are we going to have sex now?"

"No. We're going to talk." He set her on her feet, turned her toward the bathroom, and patted her bottom. "Go potty. I'll find your clothes." They were scattered all over the floor from when he'd tossed them in every direction earlier.

He watched as she timidly hurried toward the bathroom,

checking out her bottom as she went. Sure enough, the only mark on her cute ass was the slight red indentation from the bear's nose.

He hadn't been kidding about his cock. It was the hardest he'd ever experienced. Now wasn't the time to deal with it, though. He only had an hour before he needed to leave.

When Eden stepped back into the room, she had her arms crossed, and she rushed over to him. She reached for the pile of clothes on his lap when she got close enough.

"Hey, what's the hurry?"

She frowned. "I'm naked."

He tipped her chin back. "I've seen every inch of your pretty body, Ladybug. I think you can stop trying to hide from Daddy now."

She sighed when he used his other hand to set her clothes on the bed out of her reach. "Daddy..." Damn, he loved that sound. The edge of whiny. So cute.

"Lower your arms and let Daddy dress you."

She humphed this time but finally dropped her arms to her sides.

Gabriel took his time helping her into her panties before adding her leggings. He left her shirt for last because he knew it unnerved her to have her breasts exposed, but also because he was rather fond of seeing her exposed breasts.

She didn't breathe right until the shirt was in place.

Gabriel fought the urge to chuckle as he rose, lifted her onto his hip, and carried her to the living room. He sat on the couch and arranged her on his lap, straddling him. He wanted her full attention.

Holding her by the hips, he met her gaze. "I haven't asked you about your family, Ladybug. Do you have anyone in the area?"

She shook her head. "It was just my father and me. He died from an aneurysm two years ago."

"No siblings or grandparents?"

"No." She toyed with the front of his T-shirt absently.

"Where is your mother?"

She shrugged. "She took off when I was a baby. My father didn't talk about her much. I don't think she wanted kids, so she just left."

"I'm sorry, Ladybug." That was depressing.

"It's okay. I never knew her. I mean, I don't remember her. My father was a great father. He did the best he could raising me, even though he was older. I met my grandparents several times when I was young, but they both passed by the time I was ten."

So, Eden is really and truly totally on her own.

"Well, we have that in common, then. I don't have any family, either. I was raised by my aunt until I turned eighteen and joined the Army."

"How long were you in the Army?"

"Thirteen years. I was injured in an explosion five years ago. I came back to Shadowridge, found the Guardians, and knew I was home. I was a chaplain in the Army, so it was seamless that I became the chaplain for the MC."

"What do you do as a chaplain? Are you like a priest?"

He chuckled. "No, Little one. I'm more like an advisor. I keep all the records for the MC and many of the secrets. My real job is in counseling. My experience in the Army and my own PTSD led me to become a crisis operator for the veteran's hotline."

She nodded. "That must be really hard."

He shrugged. "Some days it can be. Mostly, I feel like I'm helping people, and that's what's important. Sometimes, I have to take an odd shift, even at night, but mostly, I do the scheduling and make sure all the shifts are covered. My boss, the man who runs the crisis center, is amazing."

"That's good."

He squeezed her hips. "Thank you for sharing. I wanted to

know a little more about you, and now you know more about me."

"Probably important if I'm going to stay here for a while. Do you think I'll ever be able to go back to my apartment?"

Gabriel slid his hands up her back. He wouldn't allow himself to get annoyed every time she brought this subject up. She needed him to be gentle and nurturing. "No, Ladybug. You won't be able to go back, not just because of the threat from the Devil's Jesters. I promise to put an end to that. You can't go back because you're mine, Eden," he reminded her.

"You keep saying that, but it's hard to believe you mean it."

"I know, Little one. But I'll keep telling you until, eventually, you'll know it in your heart." He set one hand over her chest and patted her. "Now, can you be brave for me while I'm gone?"

"How long will you be gone?"

"I'm not sure. Hopefully, not too long. You'll be here with Carlee and the other Little girls. A lot of my brothers will be here, including Atlas. You'll also meet Faust and Storm. Did you meet Rock earlier?"

She shook her head. "I saw him when we were in the tree. He's Atlas and Remi's father, right?"

"Yep. He's a good guy. He had a heart attack a while back, so he's learning to eat healthier. You girls should definitely tattle on him if you catch him eating junk food," he joked.

She giggled and shook her head. "There's no way I would tattle on Remi and Atlas's father."

He chuckled, grateful he'd managed to turn this conversation into something lighter. Finally, he lifted her off his lap and set her on her feet. "Go find your socks, Ladybug. I don't want your feet to get cold."

She leaned in and hugged him long and hard before turning to rush into the bedroom.

When she returned, he was waiting for her by the door. "Good girl. Can you try to stay out of trouble while I'm gone?"

She shook her head. "If you want me to make friends, then obviously, I'll need to join in the shenanigans."

He rolled his eyes. "Obviously," he said, repeating her word from earlier.

The Little imp was even batting her eyes. She was definitely going to be a handful. That was as clear as day.

CHAPTER
FOURTEEN

Gabriel wasn't usually the sort to lose his temper. He was a counselor. He was damn good at helping people who were in dire situations. He had to be the calm one when faced with a crisis. It was his job.

However, his skin was crawling as he climbed off his bike and stepped up next to Steele. He planted his feet wide and set his hands on his hips in an intimidating posture.

When the six of them had pulled up, they'd found six of the Devil's Jesters already waiting in the abandoned parking lot. They looked cocky, bored, and displeased.

"You can wipe that fucking smirk off your face," Steele growled, his gaze pinned on the man standing next to Slash.

Luckily, Slash, the Jesters' president, shot his man a glare before looking back toward the Shadowridge Guardians. "What's this all about, boys? We have plans for tonight. Let's make this quick."

Gabriel let Steele talk. It was better that way. For one thing, he wasn't sure he could control his temper. For another, these men didn't need to know that the woman four of their MC had on their radar was his own woman.

Steele was unwavering. "It would seem some of your

members have been causing trouble in town lately, specifically last night."

Slash lifted a brow and glanced around at the others. "Oh, that's news to me. Any of you know about this?"

Five men shook their heads. *Liars.*

Steele took an intimidating step closer. "Drop the act, Slash. It's not attractive. Four of your men were at the diner on the edge of town last night. They harassed the waitress, who is one of ours. On top of that, they went to her home and flipped the place. Ring a bell?"

Gabriel kept his gaze locked on the asshole next to Slash. They'd all agreed to hone in on one man each so they could catch any nuance of reaction to this conversation.

The fucker Gabriel had been assigned to, the one who'd been smirking when they'd arrived, looked down. He had definitely been involved. Gabriel wanted to strangle him until he begged for mercy.

"Anyone know anything about this accusation?" Slash asked, glancing around at his men.

Every one of them shook their head in denial. A quick glance around told Gabriel more than one was lying. They wouldn't make eye contact, and they'd lost a bit of their fucking cocky attitudes. A few faces had paled. The truth was when they'd harassed Eden and then broken into her home, they hadn't known she was under the protection of the Guardians. In truth, she hadn't been. Not then, anyway. But they couldn't have known that, and she sure as fuck was now.

Steele continued. "It would seem to me you need a come to Jesus with your club members, Slash. Four of them caused this trouble, and I'd bet my last dollar they bragged about it to most of the rest of the club, which means at least half of the men standing here with you now are lying cowards who thought it would be funny to harass a woman in town and then scare the hell out of her by breaking into her apartment and trashing it. Would you like me to tell you the message they left on her bathroom mirror?"

Slash ran a hand down his face. "Fuck." It seemed he'd been unaware of these events, and that had been fine until now. It would be his responsibility to make this right by going back to his club, taking care of the problem, and ensuring it didn't happen again.

Steele spoke again. "Just so we're clear, we know exactly who those four men are. They might have thought they were full of spit and vinegar when they conned the manager of the diner into giving them the waitress's address, but Shadowridge is *our* town. Not yours. The manager isn't exactly on my good-boy list. This isn't the first time he's caused problems. However, he had no choice but to switch his loyalty from your men to mine this morning, if you get my drift. When your men come to town to eat, or for any other reason, they need to start exercising respect for the citizens. As well, it wouldn't matter if that waitress was under our protection or not. We won't tolerate your club scaring people in town. Do I make myself clear?"

Slash glared at Steele with narrowed eyes. "You threatening me, asshole?"

"Nope, I'm making a suggestion. And before your men decide to retaliate against the manager of the diner, consider the fact that there were at least eight other patrons in the diner who could have told us which four of your men had been in last night. They weren't subtle in their harassment. They were loud, rude, and crude. They disturbed the peace with their vile comments and disgusting behavior."

Slash's nostrils flared as he continued to shoot daggers at the Guardians. He set his hands on his hips. "I'll get to the bottom of it. You have my word."

"I expect you to keep that word. I won't have one of my women afraid to leave the compound without always looking over her shoulder. I'll give you forty-eight hours to clean up your garden, and then I expect to hear good news from you."

Slash gave a nod, turned around, and headed for his bike. His men followed, and the six of them pulled out of the parking lot before any of the Guardians moved a muscle.

"I think we shook him up," King stated.

"I sure fucking hope so," Gabriel added. "I don't know what that asshole is going to do, but if my Little girl is stuck living in fear for much longer, I can't promise I'll remain non-violent."

Steele nodded. "Understood. Let's go."

Gabriel was fuming as he mounted his bike and took off behind Steele. Hopefully, the wind on his face would cool him off a bit before he got back to his girl.

Unfortunately, he would have needed more like an hour to get his head straight, and the six of them were only ten minutes from the compound. There was no way Gabriel would head off on his own half-cocked to blow off steam. He didn't have that luxury any longer. He had a Little girl waiting for him. She needed him. He needed to pull his shit together and be strong for her.

Ten minutes passed quickly, and soon, they were striding back into the clubhouse. The scowl on Gabriel's face vanished the moment he took in the scene. An elaborate pile of blankets, chairs, tables, and couches had been used to build a fort. Gabriel peeked through a sliver of space between overlapping blankets to see Ivy, Remi, Harper, and Carlee in the fort with Eden. They were sitting under it, giggling like crazy.

Gabriel's heart was full. It had been one thing to watch his brothers as they found their forever Littles, but finding his own was out of this stratosphere.

Eden was his heart. His soul. *His forever.*

One day. He'd had her for only one day. He snickered inside as he thought about the times his brothers had met their Littles and fallen hard for them in a shocking few hours. He'd been doubtful about how strong a bond two people could create in such a short time—until it had happened to him. Now, he was living proof. He would never be a naysayer again.

Steele was grinning like a loon as he strode over to Rock. They all were. It was Steele who whispered, "Dare I ask if any bottoms need spanking?"

Rock smiled and shook his head. "Not a one. Angels, all of them. It might take them a while to clean up tomorrow morning, but nobody tried to hide or otherwise create mischief."

Atlas stood next to his father. "He tells the truth. Even Carlee was good." He smirked as though that was a feat in and of itself.

Gabriel quietly shuffled toward the fort before dropping onto his hands and knees and climbing into the elaborate structure.

The girls squealed when they saw him. They had brought stuffies and dolls into their domain, and they were sitting in a circle talking. Each of them had a lovie in their lap. Ivy also had a notebook in her lap, and she slapped it shut when she saw him.

"Look, Daddy!" Eden called out, holding up her ladybug stuffie. "Carlee fixed Spot while I was napping."

Gabriel didn't think his heart could take much more of her cuteness, but more importantly, she'd called him Daddy in front of all her friends. "He looks as good as new. Thank you, Carlee." He winked at the brown-eyed girl with the wavy brown pigtails.

"And you know what else?" Eden said excitedly, bouncing on her butt.

"What, Ladybug?"

"Atlas found a pot for my plant and gave it a new home. He thinks it will survive."

God bless his brothers. "I'm so glad, Little one."

"This is a girls-only fort, Uncle Gabriel," Remi told him,

waving a hand in the direction he'd crawled in. "You can't be in here."

Gabriel grinned. "But I *am* in here," he pointed out.

They all broke down in giggles.

"Well, you shouldn't be," Eden stated in agreement. She pointed at the opening. "We're talking about important secret club things."

"Ah, well, in that case…" Gabriel smiled at his Little girl as he backed carefully out of the fort. He certainly didn't want to be responsible for the collapse of any of the "walls."

Damn, his life was looking up.

CHAPTER
FIFTEEN

*T*wo *days later…*

The piercing scream radiating through his suite had Gabriel jumping up from his desk chair so fast it fell backward as he ran from his office to his bedroom.

His heart was racing as he found Eden sitting up in bed, eyes wide, breathing heavily, tears streaming down her face. "What happened, Ladybug?" he asked as he closed the distance and pulled her into his arms.

It was the middle of the night, but he'd had to work a night shift, and he'd tucked her in three hours ago.

She grabbed the front of his shirt and sniffled. "I had a nightmare."

He pulled her onto his lap and rubbed her back. "I'm so sorry, Ladybug. Do you want to talk about it?"

She shook her head, but words tumbled out anyway. "I took the bus home from work like I always do, but when I got there, that man who pinched my butt was inside, and he grabbed me as soon as I walked in the door. He put his hand over my mouth and dragged me into my bedroom." She started sobbing.

Fucking Rat. Literally. The man who had pinched her was a smarmy little asshole who went by the name of Rat. He was probably five-foot-seven and weighed one-twenty. Gabriel shook his head in disdain. It was a bold move, mistreating a waitress in a neighboring town, and even bolder, tearing her apartment to shreds.

Gabriel had considered hunting the fucker down more than one time in the past two days. Usually the calm voice of reason, it had taken Steele and Atlas to talk him off the ledge.

The forty-eight hours were up, and no one had heard from Slash. Gabriel was furious and feared that meant the Devil's Jesters had decided not to heed Steele's advice. What were the fuckers planning?

"I'm so sorry, Little one. It was a bad dream. It's over now. You're here in our suite, and you're safe." Outwardly, he hoped he was projecting calm. Inside, he was thinking of dismembering that fucking Rat.

She sniffled. "Can you come to bed now, Daddy?"

"Not yet, Ladybug. I'm sorry. I have a few more hours on my shift, and then I'll climb under the covers with you." He helped her lie back down, tucked Coco and Spot in with her, and pulled the covers up to her neck. He'd put a cute nightie on her before he'd tucked her in the first time.

He'd put a nightie on her every night so far, mostly to keep himself from mauling her. The idea had been a horrible one, though, because his Little girl was somehow just as sexy wearing the nighties as she was when she was naked.

Gabriel was struggling to keep his hands off her, and the struggle was growing by the hour. He'd had her three days now, and his cock was constantly hard. He didn't want to rush her to have sex. He wanted her to take the time to adjust to her new life and fully embrace it first.

After kissing her forehead, he rubbed her hip. "Go back to sleep, Ladybug. Before you know it, I'll be climbing in to join you." He couldn't wait. His shift was dragging on and on. Even though he'd taken a few serious calls tonight, in between, he'd been thinking of nothing but his Little girl in here in their bed without him.

"Okay, Daddy." She smiled at him.

Gabriel slipped out of the room and hurried to his office, grateful to see no missed calls. He'd feel like shit if he'd missed an incoming call. Calls in the middle of the night were usually the most important ones. People who suffered from PTSD often needed the most help late at night when demons haunted them.

After taking care of several emails and business-related tasks, he fielded one more call and then passed the baton to the guy on shift after him and headed for bed.

As he peeled off his clothes, he stared down at his Little girl. *I'm the luckiest bastard on earth.*

Down to his boxers, he pulled the covers back and climbed into bed.

"Daddy?" Eden asked sleepily.

"Right here, Ladybug." He rolled toward her and spooned her from behind, planting a kiss on her neck as he settled against her, breathing easier now that she was in his arms.

He loved that she'd started calling him Daddy even when she was barely lucid. It came naturally to her. She was fitting in at the compound better than he'd ever expected. Perhaps it helped that she'd already known Carlee and that Carlee was Little and Atlas was her Daddy. She'd had a chance to grasp the concept and wrap her head around it some before Gabriel had swooped in and claimed her.

A long, deep sigh escaped her lips, telling him she was just as relieved to be in his arms as he was to be holding her. She set her small hand over his under her breasts and gripped him. "Thank you for being my Daddy," she murmured.

"Thank you for being my Little girl," he whispered in her ear.

Another sigh, and she relaxed completely, falling back asleep.

It took Gabriel a long time to join her. His mind was racing through so many things. He'd always had trouble getting to sleep after working a night shift because it was hard to separate from the calls he'd taken. On top of that, he was worried about the Devil's Jesters. And finally, he really just wanted to stay awake and stare at the woman he was fortunate enough to have claimed as his own. How fucking lucky could he get?

It seemed like minutes passed before he roused because something was touching his cock. No. Some*one*. He didn't need to open his eyes to remember where he was and who was touching him. He could smell her shampoo, where her pretty red curls were tickling his nose.

She was also squirming against him as though cupping his morning hard-on was making her horny, too. He liked that thought. He wasn't sure how he felt about her touching his erection, however. She was making it impossible to not flatten her on her back and claim her completely once and for all.

She snuggled closer and kissed his chest. "I know you're not sleeping, Daddy."

He chuckled as he eased one hand down and covered hers, pressing it tighter against his erection. "What are you doing, naughty girl?"

"Something was poking me in the back, so I wanted to know what it was," she teased.

"Is that so? Would you also like to see it so you'll have a better understanding?"

"Yes." The one word was breathless, as if she'd expected him to turn her down and was relieved when he hadn't.

When he finally opened his eyes, he found her staring at him. Her cheeks were red, flushed from either arousal or embarrassment. "Are you sure you're ready to meet my cock, Ladybug?"

She giggled as she nodded. "You say that like it's a separate being from you. Does it have a name?"

"Definitely not, and don't get any ideas." He lifted a warning brow. He knew some Littles liked to name their Daddies' cocks. He did not want to go down that path.

She giggled again. "Okay, then maybe don't talk about your, uh, penis in the third person."

He chuckled. "I know I told you not to use bad words, but when we're in bed, you may call my erection a cock, Ladybug."

She shook her head. "You can't actually use the word Ladybug and, uh, the C word in the same sentence. It's against the rules."

His body shook as he laughed. "My bad. I didn't realize there were rules."

"Well, there are. You have rules, so I can have some, too. There's a notebook full of them, you know." She gasped, eyes going wide as she said that.

He lifted both brows. Having a full discussion with a woman's hand on his dick was a new one for him, but he thought maybe he liked this banter.

"I shouldn't have said that. Forget I did, okay?"

"Definitely not. Who has this notebook, naughty girl?"

"What notebook? You're making stuff up. There's no notebook." She shook her head and gripped his cock harder as if she could distract him.

He lifted her hand off his shaft, brought her fingers to his lips, and kissed them. "Wanna know a secret?"

She sighed. "It seems I'm not very good with secrets."

He chuckled and whispered conspiratorially, "All the Daddies know about the secret notebook. We even know that's what you were giggling about in your fort the other night. Don't worry. I won't tell anyone you leaked private girl-club information if you don't tell anyone their secret is not so secret."

She gasped again, her eyes wide. "The Daddies know?"

"Yep." He pulled her middle finger into his mouth and sucked it.

She stared at his lips and licked her own. "Have the Daddies *seen* it?" she asked, struggling to pay attention.

He released her finger with a pop. "No. They don't need to. The Littles aren't very quiet when they write in it. You do realize blanket forts are not soundproof, right?" he teased.

She swallowed. "Yeah, but…"

He held her hand in one of his and slid his other under her nightie to flatten his palm on the smooth skin of her back.

"Daddy…you're distracting me," she murmured, her eyes rolling back as he eased his fingers around and cupped her breast.

"Am I?"

She nodded, mouth falling open.

He flicked her nipple. "Are you worried the Daddies know about the naughty-word list and how the Littles like to get around using them?"

Her breath hitched.

"Maybe you're worried the Daddies will find out about planned pranks, the nicknames you naughty girls have for some of us, or where you have hidden stashes of candy, hmmm?" He pushed her nightie over her head, leaned in, and sucked her nipple before she could respond.

A deep moan escaped her lips, pleasing him immensely. He didn't care about the notebook. None of the Daddies cared. They all thought it was humorous. It was all in good fun. Mostly silliness.

After switching his attention to her other nipple, he finally lifted his head to stare down at his sexy Little girl's body. "I could look at you all day," he whispered as he reverently circled one of her nipples until it was tight and swollen.

"Will you make love to me now, Daddy?"

He smoothed his hand up her chest until he reached her cheek. He wanted to pause and make sure she was ready for this step. "Are you certain, Ladybug? We don't have to have sex if you're not ready yet."

"I'm not a virgin, Daddy," she retorted.

"That may be, but in a lot of ways, you're more innocent than if you were a virgin, Eden."

She scrunched up her nose. "How do you figure that?"

"Because not knowing what sex might be like is very different from thinking it's something it's not. Your three horrible boyfriends have caused you to have a very warped vision of sex in your head. It's not going to be like that. It's going to be fireworks and lightning bolts. You sure you're ready for that?"

"Daddy...you're exaggerating."

"Mmm. You want to find out?"

She nodded. "Yes."

He leaned forward and kissed her. He didn't stop kissing her until she melted beneath him, let her head tip to one side to allow him to penetrate deeper, and eventually moaned into his mouth.

She was panting when he released her lips. "Please..."

Gabriel rolled away from her to open the drawer on the nightstand and grab a condom. He'd purchased them two days ago, so he'd be prepared when the time was right.

Lifting his hips, he shrugged out of his boxers and rolled the condom down his length. "Climb on top of me, Ladybug."

She rose slowly onto her hip so she could look down at him. "You want me on top?" she asked hesitantly.

"To start. Don't worry." He leaned over, grabbed her hips,

and lifted her so that she straddled him. When he lowered her, his cock flattened against his stomach, lodged between her lower lips.

She set her hands on his chest to support herself. Her mouth was hanging open. "Oh."

"Rub yourself against my cock, Little one," he encouraged. He had two goals here. One was that he wanted her to take her pleasure on him so she would feel empowered. Two was that he wanted to fucking watch her. She was so damn gorgeous.

She leaned farther forward, supporting herself with her palms closer to his shoulders. Her tits were the sexiest he'd ever seen or even dreamed of. Creamy white, exactly the right size, with small pink nipples. The splattering of freckles just made her even more gorgeous.

Eden let herself go, eyes rolling back as she eased her slit back and forth over his cock. "Mmmm."

He smiled, watching her breasts sway, glancing down at their connection every so often. Her hair was a mess of curls that made her look so damn sweet. It tumbled over her shoulders. She would want him to braid it later because she'd decided she liked it best that way, but at night, he always took it down so he could run his fingers through it and see her like this in the morning.

When he reached for her nipples and gave them a slight pinch, she moaned. "I'm gonna come..."

"That's the idea," he teased.

She whimpered. "Daddy..."

He cupped her breasts and let them sway and bounce in his light grip. "Rock your clit against my cock, Ladybug. Make yourself come, and then I'll flip you onto your back and push my erection into you."

She arched her neck, panting now, picking up speed as if she could finally permit herself to come now that she knew the entire plan.

She was so wanton and uninhibited, and he knew at that

moment he loved her. She was perfection. She was about to be his in every way.

Rocking herself forward, she found her rhythm. Her eyes were partially closed. Her mouth was tipped up in a slight smile. He knew she was about to come. He'd grown used to the signs, and he loved being able to read her.

Even though he hadn't had his cock inside her yet, nor had he let her touch it before this morning, he'd made her come at least once every day. He'd wanted her to learn that it would always be that way between them. He'd wanted to erase the weird experiences she'd had with bad lovers in the past until she believed that it would forever be only amazing with him.

Her breath hitched, and she rubbed harder right before she gasped and then panted through her orgasm. Even though he was already wearing a condom, he could feel her cream sliding down around his erection to drip onto his pelvis.

Heaven.

CHAPTER
SIXTEEN

E den was trembling as she opened her eyes to meet Gabriel's gaze. He was smiling at her, mostly supporting her with his hands on her waist. Otherwise, she might have fallen to one side while she'd been out of her mind.

She gave him a shy smile. "That was nice."

He chuckled. "I bet I can make it even better."

She squealed as he flipped her onto her back and landed between her spread thighs. "Daddy!"

He kissed her again in that way that caused all her molecules to divide so that she lost track of the day and what her name was. When he lifted his head, she was dizzy.

His erection was lodged against her opening, and she lifted her hips, hoping to encourage him.

He cupped her face. "Are you sure, Ladybug? We don't have to have sex yet if you're not ready."

"Daddy...I'm certain." She ran her hands up and down his muscular back as she wrapped her legs around his waist and tipped her hips so that she could get better contact. His erection slid partly in, making her breath hitch.

"Eyes on mine, Little one."

She met his gaze and smiled. "I want this, Gabriel."

That must have been all he needed because he thrust forward, filling her, making her eyes roll back. How did he think she would be able to keep her gaze on his?

He groaned deeply as he took her mouth again.

Her channel pulsed around his enormous shaft, clenching over and over from the shock of being stretched so far. It was like tiny orgasms over and over.

When he released her lips, she was panting. So was he. She'd never felt this close to another human being. He was covering her like a blanket, his face inches from hers, his hands on her head, his erection so deep. It felt so good.

"You okay, Ladybug?"

She nodded. "Do it again."

He smiled and obliged her, easing out and thrusting back in deeper.

She moaned. Nothing could have prepared her for this. It was so much better than anything she'd experienced in the past. The room was spinning out of control as he slid in and out, never losing eye contact.

Gabriel was the most intense man she'd ever met, and he was inside her, filling her so good. Suddenly, he angled his hips a bit, and the base of his shaft pressed against her clit. Sparks ignited as she dug her heels into his thighs. "Ohh..."

He did it again and again until she gasped, stunned to find herself reaching yet another peak. The orgasm that consumed her shook her to her core. Her channel gripped him tighter as he pistoned in and out.

Waves of her release kept going, or maybe she had another orgasm, but it didn't stop until Gabriel growled low and deep, fully seated inside her, his hips pulsing with his release.

When he finally relaxed his body and set his forehead against hers, he was grinning. "Eden..." The one word was reverent and so very sweet.

"Gabriel..." She let her hands roam around his back and

butt cheeks, wanting him to stay where he was forever. She didn't care that it was difficult to breathe. She never wanted him to move.

He kissed her forehead and then all over her face until she giggled. When he finally rose off her, easing out of her at the same time, he remained on his hands and knees above her, looking down. "I want to wrap you in bubble wrap and keep you in this room forever."

"Are you saying I'm clumsy?" she joked.

He chuckled. "No. I'm saying I can't stand the idea of you being anywhere except where I can see you. I had no idea I would feel so possessive and overprotective. I don't even want you to walk. I think I'll carry you everywhere from now on."

She giggled. "I don't think that's very realistic. Besides, eventually, I need to get a new job."

"Or not…"

She narrowed her gaze at him. "I can't just live in your suite and mooch off you forever, Gabriel."

"You're not mooching. You're my girl. I can take care of you."

"I'm very aware you can take care of me, but I also need to be able to take care of myself."

His brows were furrowed. "Couldn't you maybe just find some hobbies? You could read and color and play."

She shook her head. "I've been doing that for two days. I can't do it forever. Besides, what if something happened to you, and then I wasn't independent enough to take care of myself."

He growled. "Nothing is going to happen to me, and if it did, I will have ensured you were taken care of for life."

She swallowed and reached for his face. "That's intense, Gabriel. You've only known me a few days."

"I knew you were mine in a few minutes, Ladybug. I didn't need a few days. Every day, I know it even more deeply than the previous day."

"Okay," she murmured softly. His intensity was very sweet. "But I still need a job. I like working."

"Did you ever consider going to college?"

She rolled her eyes. "Sure, but then I considered robbing a bank to pay for it, and that seemed like a bad idea, so I got a job instead."

He rolled his eyes. "Sassy girl. Will you at least wait until I'm certain the Devil's Jesters are no longer a threat to you? And then maybe you could look into something you could do from home. Something that would allow me to be able to see you while you work."

She wanted to laugh at how possessive he was, but he was dead serious, too, and she didn't want to make fun of his need to protect her. Some people might have felt smothered by the way Gabriel constantly growled about her safety, but Eden felt cherished, and she needed to find a way to take care of her needs without upsetting his basic protective instinct. "Okay."

He kissed her again, then rose off the bed to waltz into the attached bath. The man was ripped. Even his ass had firm muscles. And his erection bobbed in front of him, seemingly just as hard as it had been before he'd orgasmed.

When he returned a minute later, the condom was gone, his shaft was still just as hard and exposed, and he was holding a wet washcloth. "Spread your legs for me, Ladybug. Let me clean you up."

She flushed as she reached for the cloth. "I can do it."

He held it out of her grasp. "Daddy will do it."

She sighed and relaxed into the bed. There was no use arguing with the man. He liked taking care of her, and it was easier to let him do so. Plus, if she were honest with herself, it felt nice—if she could just stop feeling so self-conscious every time he took care of her naked body.

Gabriel's phone vibrated on the nightstand, and he glanced at it before looking back at her. "I'd rather snuggle back under the covers with you and get more sleep, but that's going to be Steele, and I need to talk to some of my brothers."

"About the Jesters?"

"Yes." He found her two stuffies, tucked them in her arms, and pulled the covers back over her. "You can go back to sleep if you want, Ladybug." He headed for the drawers and grabbed a pair of boxer briefs.

She watched as he stepped into them and then pulled on jeans. He was so sexy. Every inch of him. She barely blinked while he put on a shirt, socks, and black biker boots. He gathered his hair in a bun at the back of his head next, and by then, she was nearly drooling.

He glanced at her and chuckled. "How was the show? It seemed rather boring to me."

"Not even close. Take all that off and do it again."

He laughed, planted his hands on either side of her, and kissed her briefly. "It's early. You can stay right here all warm. I'll bring you a smoothie in a bit."

"Mmm. I love your smoothies."

"Good. I'll happily make them for you as often as you want."

She'd come to realize that Gabriel was an amazing cook. He did a lot of the cooking in the compound. Bear often made breakfast, but Gabriel was usually the main contributor to dinner.

Eden stared at the door after he left, feeling blessed. She should get up and maybe take a shower...and then do what? She was more well-rested than she'd been in years. She'd been working the early shift at the diner five days a week for a long time. Sleeping in was a luxury. Until now.

She couldn't keep up this life of leisure forever. She would get bored. She needed to find something that interested her, preferably something that paid a salary. No matter how much Gabriel insisted he didn't need her to work, *she* needed it for herself.

Surely, there was something she could do that would make her feel valuable while keeping her Daddy from panicking. His idea of her working from home sounded perfect, but what would she do?

At least she didn't need to worry about it today. She was a very lucky Little girl. After a few deep cleansing breaths, she closed her eyes and hugged her stuffies tighter.

CHAPTER
SEVENTEEN

"Please tell me you've heard from Slash," Gabriel said to Steele as he entered the kitchen.

Bear handed him a cup of coffee. Kade was sipping his, leaning against the counter. Talon wandered in at the same time as Gabriel.

Steele ran a hand over his head. "Yep, and you're not going to like it. According to Slash, he's spoken with three of the guys who were at the diner that night. They insist they were only teasing Eden in good fun."

Gabriel's growl was so loud it was a wonder it didn't rattle the windows.

Steele continued, "They say Rat was the one who pinched Eden and lost his shit when she threw soda in his face. According to them, Rat is an asshole and deserved it. They knew he followed Marv to the back after Eden left, but they weren't aware Marv had given Rat her address, and they didn't leave the diner with him. They had no knowledge of him breaking into Eden's apartment and trashing the place. No one has seen Rat since that night."

"Fuck," Gabriel muttered. "And we're supposed to believe them?"

Steele sighed. "For now, I don't see how we have a choice."

"This won't help Eden feel safe. There's no way I can let her leave this compound with Rat on the loose and the rest of the guys taking no responsibility for harassing her."

"We all agree with you on that," Kade said. "I would never let Remi leave this building under these circumstances."

"But we can't go on like this forever," Bear pointed out.

Talon nodded. "I agree. We need to be on the lookout for Rat. If he hasn't been back to the clubhouse since that night, he's probably lurking somewhere, looking for Eden."

Gabriel set his mug down. It was either that or throw it across the room and create a mess of coffee and broken plaster. "Eden already thinks I'm overprotective. She's not going to like me mandating she can't leave the clubhouse, not even to go out back."

Kade nodded. "We'll all make sure one of our Littles visits her often and keeps her occupied."

Gabriel drew in a deep breath and looked around the kitchen. "I think today is a good day for sushi."

Talon winced. "Gross, and what brought that up?"

"It takes a long time to prepare; it'll keep my mind occupied, and I can enlist Eden to help me to keep her busy, too."

"I'm not eating raw fish," Talon grumbled. "I hate when you declare sushi night."

"Not all sushi has raw fish," Bear pointed out. "Gabriel always makes a mean California roll."

Talon rolled his eyes and wandered out of the kitchen.

"You're really going to let me help?" Eden asked excitedly. She was bouncing on her feet that afternoon as Gabriel told her about sushi night.

"Yes, Ladybug. You can help Daddy with the sushi rolls. No knives. No stoves. Just the rolls," he warned her.

She glared at him, hands on her hips. "You do realize that, underneath pretending I'm a Little girl most of the time, I'm a grown adult. I've been using knives and the stove for twenty years."

He grabbed her around the waist and kissed her. "You do realize I'm the Daddy in this relationship and a very overprotective one at that. No knives. No open flames. If you don't obey me in the kitchen, I'll make you stand in the corner while I cook."

Her eyes went wide. "Like a timeout?"

"Yep, and if you get sassy with me, I'll spank you first. Do you want to stand in the corner of the kitchen with a sore bottom this afternoon?"

She shook her head so fast her braids went flying and whipped him in the face. "No, Sir."

He chuckled as he caught her head to keep from getting slapped by her hair again. He also couldn't resist kissing her yet again. "Ready?" He took her hand and guided her to the kitchen.

No one was around. Most of the members and their Littles were at their day jobs. Gabriel had always liked this time of day when he could work on dinner without interruption. If a member needed him for advice or counseling, they knew they could come to him in the kitchen and either talk there or set something up for another time.

Gabriel was looking forward to having Eden with him today. She brought so much light to his life. It would never be boring again, that was for sure. "Do you like sushi, Ladybug?"

"I've only tried it a few times, but I liked it. I didn't know people made it themselves."

"It can be fun. I'll get the rice started and cut up everything, then I'll teach you how to roll it into the seaweed."

Eden looked excited, and she watched intently while he did all the prep work.

"We'll make three kinds of rolls," he told her as soon as the rice was ready. "Can you help Daddy spread the rice onto the seaweed?"

"Yes."

He did the first one to show her how thick the layer should be. "Be sure you don't press it too tight. It can be loose."

While she did that, he cut up salmon, cucumbers, carrots, cream cheese, and avocado. It took them a while, but eventually, they had plenty of rolls ready.

When the rolls were done, he set her up with colored pencils and plenty of paper. "You can draw me a picture while I finish making dinner."

Gabriel made a hot and sour soup, fried rice, and sweet and sour chicken.

"Wow, you're an amazing chef," Eden said as he wiped his hands on his apron. "I'm pretty good at following a recipe, but you did most of that off the top of your head."

He chuckled. "I do it often. I enjoy cooking. It helps me relieve stress."

"You know what you could try instead of cooking to relieve stress?" she asked. Her expression was mischievous.

"Dare I ask?" He expected her to suggest something sexual.

What she said was not sexual. "You could get your bottom spanked. I've heard it's a great stress reliever."

He laughed. "I suspect you know that firsthand by now, huh, Ladybug?"

She squirmed on her chair and shrugged before lifting the picture she'd drawn. It was of a ladybug.

"I love it. We can hang it in our suite."

She stared at him, grinning.

"What?"

"It's just so weird when you refer to your apartment as 'our' suite."

He grabbed her out of the chair and pulled her against him. "It is *ours*, Ladybug." He rained kisses all over her face.

Suddenly, the room filled with voices as several of the men came into the clubhouse.

"Damn, it smells good in here," Talon said as he leaned over the stove. "Thank God you made more than just sushi. I was worried."

Eden helped Gabriel set the long table while Gabriel carried over platters of food, and within ten minutes, the kitchen was filled with hungry men and Little girls.

As soon as they were seated, Talon leaned over the rolls. "Which one of these doesn't have raw fish?"

Gabriel pointed toward the platter of rolls closest to his end of the table.

Eden lifted her gaze to Gabriel, her mouth opening.

He winked at her and held a finger to his lips.

Eden pursed her lips while Gabriel took her plate and filled it with food.

Gabriel watched Talon out of the corner of his eye while he prepared a small dish of soy sauce, wasabi, and ginger. He held his breath as Talon took his first bite.

"Damn, that's good," Talon said as he swallowed. "What's in this one?"

"Raw salmon," Gabriel told him.

"*What*?" Talon jumped up from his seat.

Everyone else in the room laughed.

"I guess you don't hate raw fish as much as you thought," Steele pointed out before shoving a bite into his mouth. "Mmm. Delicious."

Talon took a huge drink of water. "You tricked me."

"I was just making a point," Gabriel teased.

"I'll get you back for this stunt," Talon warned him as he sat back in his chair. "Raw fish... Gross." He examined the next bite from the same roll closer, shrugged, and dipped it in the sauce.

Eden started giggling as he ate it. All the other Littles did, too.

Harper leaned over to Eden and said, "Why do the Daddies get to play pranks on each other with no repercussions? If we did something like that, we'd get our bottoms spanked."

Talon lifted his fork to point across the table in their direction. "Oh, there will be repercussions someday. Just wait. I'll think of something good."

CHAPTER
EIGHTEEN

"W here are you going?" Daddy shouted as Eden ran past him toward the door of his suite. He had been in his office, but now he was standing in the doorway.

Eden had her hand on the knob as she turned to face him. "Don't panic. I'm not leaving the planet, just the room."

"Why?" He frowned.

This man seriously did not like her out of his sight, and she was rarely apart from him. He hadn't worked many hours since she'd met him, just a few shifts now and then when he was needed. But it had been ten days, and Eden was growing a bit stir-crazy.

She hoped he wouldn't stop her from joining the other girls in the common room. "Carlee's here. She texted me. Some of the girls are going to play a game."

Gabriel stared at her for a few seconds, making her fear he would tell her no.

"Daddy," she whined. "Please, can I go play with the girls? I'll still be in the building. I promise."

He drew in a breath and ran a hand down his face as if realizing he was being unreasonable. "Of course. Be good.

Don't run. And don't you dare go outside, not even on the grounds of the compound."

"I won't." She darted back toward him and wrapped her arms around him to hug him. "If we do anything naughty, we'll do it inside the clubhouse," she joked, hoping to soften him up.

"Or, you could just stay here, and I could spank you preemptively for your sassy attitude." He lifted a brow.

She shifted her weight back and forth. Her Daddy had spanked her about every other day. She knew he would do it more often if he weren't so worried about injuring her, but part of his overprotectiveness included worrying about how hard and how often he swatted her bottom. He also liked to check it several times in the hours after he spanked her.

The thing was that Eden secretly liked the spankings and the attention afterward. Sometimes, he could be overbearing and drive her bonkers—like now—but she hadn't had anyone pay this close attention to her or care this much in years. It felt good. She liked it.

Eden had learned several things about herself since she'd arrived here. One was that as skeptical as she'd been about the concept of being spanked, it was just as he'd described it. It helped her relieve her anxiety. It also made her horny. That part was weird, but Daddy said it was common.

Another thing she'd learned was that getting into harmless trouble with the other Little girls was so much fun. It was freeing to be silly and laugh with her friends, especially knowing afterward she would be over her Daddy's knees with his palm on her bare bottom.

And then there were the naked aspects of this lifestyle. It still embarrassed her to be exposed, even to Gabriel. She felt self-conscious and nervous every time he gazed at her naked body as though perhaps, eventually, he would realize she wasn't all that and decide he was tired of her.

Her thoughts on that subject were irrational, and he'd told

her so over and over, but she couldn't stop herself from thinking negative thoughts. At least they didn't happen as often as they had in the beginning. She was learning to trust him.

The strange thing was that her embarrassment fueled her arousal. The two were intertwined. When he pulled her pants and panties down to her knees to spank her, she got horny. When he undressed her to give her a bath, she got horny. When he made her stand in the corner with her red bottom on display, she almost couldn't remain upright. Her legs grew wobbly from the mortification, but he also made her keep her feet parted wide, and the only thing she could focus on was the wetness leaking down her thighs.

He knew it, too, and that embarrassed her further, creating a vicious cycle that was beyond wackadoodle.

Even now, as she leaned into him, setting her chin on his chest to stare into his eyes, batting hers repeatedly to win him over, her panties dampened, and her nipples tightened.

She licked her dry lips. "How about if you let me go play with my friends while you finish working, and then you can spank me for whatever naughty things we think up?"

He chuckled. "Ladybug, you do realize Little girls don't ordinarily tell their Daddies when they intend to be naughty ahead of time, right?"

She shrugged. "Maybe I'm not like other Little girls."

"That's for sure." He bent his knees, lifted her, and held her against him with his huge palms under her bottom.

She wrapped her legs around his waist and threaded her fingers in his curls. "If I promise to be good and not do anything naughty, will you let me go play?"

He chuckled again and kissed her nose. "Ladybug, I'll let you go play no matter what you do. I just like you near me. I feel anxious when you're not," he admitted.

"Because you're lovestruck and can't stand to be parted from me? Or because you're worried about that Rat guy coming after me?" She knew it was a combination of both, but she wanted to voice it so he would realize she understood. Plus, it might help him relax a bit if he heard it out loud.

He didn't answer her. Instead, he groaned and playfully nibbled on her neck before setting her down. He turned her toward the door and patted her bottom. "Be good."

She skipped toward the door and turned back to look at him. "Thank you, Daddy."

"No running," he admonished.

"Skipping isn't running. It's skipping." Before he could respond, she slid out the door and closed it. Luckily, he didn't yank it back open and make her come back inside.

Eden skipped to the common room, ignoring Bear when he shouted out, "No running!"

She giggled as she kept skipping past him until she caught up with Ivy, Carlee, Remi, and Harper in the common room.

"Oh, good," Ivy exclaimed. "I was afraid Gabriel wouldn't let you join us."

Eden rolled her eyes. "You and me both. It was a close call. I'm pretty sure I agreed to getting spanked for whatever we do afterward."

They all giggled and rushed into the library to pull out a game.

Eden knew that all the girls had been told to entertain her and help keep her mind off her problems since she wasn't permitted to leave the compound. She didn't mind because it was giving her a chance to get to know everyone better, and she loved all of them. They were the best friends ever.

Plus, the Daddies weren't wrong. It was stressful knowing the man who'd threatened her presumably hadn't been seen since that night. She also knew there were two theories on that subject. It was possible Rat had indeed skipped town, and no one knew where he was. But it was also possible that Slash had lied and knew exactly where Rat was hiding. Neither of those options was better than the other. And how long was this going to go on?

Gabriel told her ten times a day not to step one foot outside the clubhouse. She always sassed him in return, but the truth was she had no interest in stepping outside. The thought scared her at least as much as it did him.

For the next two hours, Eden enjoyed several board games with her friends, and then they decided to play red light, green light in the common room.

When they stepped out of the library area, no one was looking, so they put a taped line on the floor on one side of the room and pushed all the chairs out of the way.

They played rock, paper, scissors to determine who would be the leader first, and Ivy won. She raced across the room and stepped up onto a chair to see better.

In the back of her mind—no, that wasn't true; it was right in the forefront—Eden knew this game would get them all in trouble. But she didn't care. They were having fun. Plus, they needed some exercise.

"Green light," Ivy yelled.

The rest of them raced forward as fast as they could.

"Red light!"

They all came to a stop. Except Carlee. She tumbled onto the floor, laughing uproariously.

Ivy pointed at her. "You're out."

Carlee was still giggling as Ivy resumed. "Green light!"

Eden, Remi, and Harper took off again, but a second later, Eden tripped over her own feet and landed on her butt. "Ouch." She tried to get up, but her ankle hurt, making her wince.

Harper kneeled beside her immediately. "Uh oh. Did you twist your ankle?"

"I guess so." Eden winced as she tried to move it.

"I'll get my Daddy," Harper said, scrambling to her feet.

"What's going on in here?" came a bellowing voice that

belonged to Bear. When he saw them huddled on the floor, he rushed forward and dropped to a knee. "Did you fall?"

Eden nodded. She had her lips pursed, trying not to cry. Her ankle was starting to throb.

Bear gently took her leg and lifted it. "Doc will be here in a second, Little one. Remi, can you go get Gabriel? Carlee, how about if you get one of the ice packs from the freezer? Ivy, will you let Steele know what happened?"

Everyone took off, leaving Eden with Bear. She liked Bear. A lot. He was very kind and made great pancakes, but he wasn't her Daddy, and tears started to fall.

"It's okay, Little one. I promise. Probably just a sprain."

The only sound in the room for several seconds was her sniffling, and then it filled with voices as both her Daddy and Doc arrived at the same time, followed by all the girls, Carlee holding an ice pack.

Gabriel scooped her right off the floor, being careful not to jostle her leg. "Did you twist it, Ladybug?" His voice was tight.

She nodded, not wanting to cry in front of everyone.

Doc leaned over her ankle and said, "Let's get you into my office."

Gabriel followed Doc down the long hallway to Doc's office. "It's going to be okay, Ladybug. Take a breath."

She tried to breathe, but she couldn't because then she would cry.

Luckily, Doc had taken the ice from Carlee, and only Doc, Eden, and Gabriel entered the medical room. As soon as Doc shut the door, Eden let out a long breath and started crying softly. "It hurts, Daddy."

"I know, Ladybug." He sat her gently on the exam table. Eden had only peeked into this room so far. She hadn't wanted to look closer because it was a scary doctor's office, just like the kind she'd been to as a child. It had an exam table, a wall of cabinets, and a long counter with all sorts of things on it she'd rather not think about.

Doc pulled up a rolling stool and sat next to her foot. He gently took it in his hands. "Tell me when it hurts, Little one."

She cried out when he turned it.

"I'm sorry, Eden," he said before twisting it carefully in the other direction.

That side didn't hurt as badly. She only winced.

When he pressed it forward, she whimpered. When he pushed her toes toward her shin, she cried out again. "Owie!"

Gabriel looked pale. She knew she was freaking him out. He was actually holding it together pretty well, considering how badly she could feel his heart racing against her. After all, he was plastered to her side. He was also gripping her hand too tightly, but she didn't mention that. She was squeezing his just as hard.

"It hurts, Daddy," she whimpered. She tipped her head back to look at him. "I'm sorry I was naughty." She started crying harder and leaned her face into his chest.

He rubbed her back and kissed the top of her head. "It's okay, Little one. All that matters is that you're okay."

"I suspect it's just a sprain," Doc said, "but I'd take her to the urgent care in town to get an X-ray just in case. I'm going to take your shoe off and wrap this ice around it, Little one, to keep it from swelling."

"Be brave for me, Ladybug," Daddy said.

Eden sucked in a breath and held it, gritting her teeth while Doc carefully removed her tennis shoe and then held the ice up to the outside of her ankle before wrapping an ace bandage around it. "Her leggings and sock will keep the ice from getting too close to her skin. This will be fine for now. How about I drive your SUV, and you sit in the back with Eden?"

"That would be great. Thank you," Gabriel said.

Eden flinched when she heard the distinct sound of a pill bottle, and when she looked toward Doc, she saw him tipping it over to shake two pills into his hand. "This is just a painkiller, Little girl. It will dull the ache. Let me get you a juice box." He turned around, squatted in front of a small refrigerator, and pulled out a juice box.

Eden was grateful because she was also thirsty. She didn't really like to swallow pills, but these weren't too large, and she didn't want to argue with either Doc or her Daddy about taking them, so she bravely put them in her mouth and swallowed them down with the juice.

"Good girl. Let's go get that X-ray now," Gabriel said as he lifted her off the table and cradled her in his arms.

CHAPTER
NINETEEN

"We're home," Doc declared two hours later as he pulled the SUV up to the clubhouse.

"Shit," Gabriel said under his breath as he stared out the window. At the same time, Eden heard the rev of engines approaching.

Doc stopped the SUV at the entrance and turned off the engine. "Devil's Jesters?" he surmised.

Eden's breath hitched. She'd hoped the arriving bikes were members of their own MC. She twisted her neck around to watch as three bikes pulled up along the street and parked.

"Do not move from this spot, understood?" Gabriel told her unnecessarily.

She nodded. His warning was equally unnecessary since her ankle was sprained, swollen, and wrapped—in addition to the fact that she'd been told not to put any weight on it.

Gabriel jumped down from the SUV at the same time as Doc. He left the door open, thankfully.

Several other club members came out of the clubhouse and from the bike shop, crowding into the street as the three men pulled off their helmets.

Eden's eyes went wide. She knew those guys. They were

three of the men who had harassed her that night at the diner. What were they doing here? Surely, they wouldn't harm her in broad daylight in front of so many people.

"What are you doing here, Vengeance?" Gabriel snarled. Apparently, he knew at least one of them by name.

The man, who must have been named Vengeance, held up both hands even though he was scowling. "We're unarmed. You can pull back your muscle, Gabriel."

Gabriel looked larger than life with his chest pumped forward and his hands on his hips. "You're not welcome here. This better be good."

Vengeance lowered his arms, but his eyes were narrowed. "The three of us were at the diner that night with Rat. We just wanted to come by and tell your woman we meant her no harm."

Eden flinched.

Vengeance continued, "Slash doesn't want any bad blood with y'all."

"So, he made you come here to apologize?" Steele asked as he stepped closer to Gabriel.

Eden could barely see the men now. As more of the Guardians joined the commotion, they mostly blocked her view. Intentionally, she was certain. They were all protecting her.

"Basically," Vengeance continued. He may have been forced to come give a half-hearted apology, but his voice indicated he wasn't happy about it. "Listen, Rat is not a good guy. He likes to cause a commotion. I swear we didn't know he had gotten your woman's address and gone to her apartment, though. He's been voted out of the MC. He won't be welcomed back. The rest of us wanted to assure your woman we have no beef with her."

"That's all well and good, but none of you have a fucking clue where Rat is, do you?" Gabriel ground out.

"Unfortunately, no. We still haven't seen him."

"So, the fact that he's been voted out doesn't really help my woman, nor does it make her any safer, does it?"

"No."

Eden was sure Gabriel and the rest of his brothers were not pleased, but at least these three seemed relatively sincere.

Steele cleared his throat. "For all we know, you three are just blowing hot air so we'll let our guard down. If that's the case, you can let Slash know we will never let our guard down when it comes to our women. It would be best if you all assumed that every woman in this town is one of ours. Safer that way. Don't harass anyone, and you won't accidentally piss us the fuck off. Because if anything happens to any one of ours, there will be hell to pay. Take that back to Slash."

Eden couldn't see the men at all now, but she assumed they must have nodded.

The one called Vengeance spoke again. "You'll give your woman our apologies?"

"I will," Gabriel responded curtly.

A moment later, the engines roared to life again, and the three bikes peeled away from the curb.

Gabriel waited until they were long gone before he turned around and hurried over to the SUV. He gently lifted Eden out of the car and kissed her forehead, but he didn't say a word as he carried her into the clubhouse.

Eden was a smart girl. She knew he was barely controlling his anger by a thread. He didn't want it to leak out in front of her, but she was also a big girl, and she could take it.

She waited until they were in the bedroom and he was lowering her to the bed before she spoke. "It's okay, Daddy. I know you're furious. You don't have to hide it."

He drew a deep breath and kissed her cheek, letting his lips linger there for long moments before pulling back. "How did you get so smart?"

She shrugged and grabbed his neck. Sobering, she asked, "Are you mad at me?"

He frowned. "No, Ladybug, I'm not mad at you." He sat on the edge of the bed and grabbed all the pillows to pile up behind her and under her leg to elevate her ankle.

"But I was naughty," she argued.

He shrugged. "Part of being Little is the naughtiness. It's expected. I didn't really think you were going to meet up with the other girls and not get into trouble."

"But I was running, and I fell, and you hate it when I run." She watched him closely, trying to figure out what his mood was underneath his obvious stress about what had happened out front just now.

He smiled. "Eden, you're my Little girl, and you always will be. I'll likely always be hovering and overprotective, too. It's in my nature. However, under your Little persona is a grown adult, as you like to remind me from time to time, and that means you're capable of making choices. Today, one of them meant you twisted your ankle." He shrugged. "People twist their ankles. Shit happens. In a few weeks, you'll be as good as new."

"I bet you're not sorry I'm not allowed to put any weight on it for a week," she muttered.

"Not one bit." He grinned broadly. "You'll stay right here where I can see you. If you need to be somewhere else, I'll carry you there. Next week, Doc can start you on exercises to help your recovery. It's going to be sore. That will be enough of a punishment for running in the clubhouse."

Eden worried her hands together. "Do you think those Jester guys were telling the truth? They won't bother me?"

Gabriel nodded. "Yes. If they did bother you, there would be hell to pay, and they know it. I'm sure Slash sent them to make peace. I don't trust the Devil's Jesters to stay out of town and stop causing trouble, but they wouldn't dare harass you again."

"But they don't know where Rat is…"

"Right. That's the biggest problem."

"Maybe he left town."

"Maybe, but that doesn't make me feel warm and fuzzy." He squeezed her hand. "I'm sorry this is happening, Ladybug, but until I'm sure Rat is out of the picture, I will never feel comfortable letting you leave the property on your own."

"I understand, Daddy, and don't worry. I wouldn't want to, either. I'd be too scared."

He stared at her. "You're my life."

She threw her arms around him and hugged him tight. "I love you, Daddy." She stiffened and gasped as those words left her mouth. They hadn't declared their love yet, even though she'd thought it often.

He leaned her back and met her gaze. "I love you, too, Eden. So very much." He lifted her fingers to his lips and kissed her knuckles.

She smiled so big it hurt her face. "Will you make me one of your smoothies?"

"It would be my pleasure. Will you promise not to move from this bed?"

"Yes, Daddy."

He narrowed his gaze. "Not even to go to the bathroom, understood? If you need to go, I will carry you to the toilet."

"You're not going to watch me pee, Daddy." She curled up her nose.

"Mmm. We'll see." He stood and kissed her before backing out of the room. "Be right back with your smoothie."

CHAPTER
TWENTY

Four nights later, Gabriel awoke to the sound of his phone ringing. He lunged to grab it off the nightstand, glancing at the clock to see that it was just after midnight. Who would be calling at this hour?

Sitting up, he looked at the screen. It was Doc.

"Doc? Aren't you on shift with the fire department?"

"Yes. King is with me. We're still here on the site of a fire. It was a four-alarm out of town, but we got called to help. It's almost out now. I'm sorry to wake you, but you're going to want to hear this."

"What?" Gabriel glanced at Eden, who had risen to sit next to him. She looked concerned.

"It was the Devil's Jesters' clubhouse."

Gabriel gasped. "Are you serious?"

"Yes. Arson. Guess who started the fire?"

Gabriel stiffened. "Rat?"

"Got it in one. He doused one of the outbuildings with gasoline and lit up the sky. The prick jumped on his bike to flee the scene, but a few of the other club members were returning from a night out and caught him. They wrestled him to the ground, called 911, and held him until the police and the fire department arrived."

"Please tell me he was arrested." Gabriel grabbed Eden's hand and met her gaze. There was a good chance she could hear all of this just fine in the silence of the room.

"He was. I have to get back to make sure there are no injuries. My shift ends in the morning. I'll get as many details as possible and share them with you when I arrive."

"Thank you, and thanks for calling. You're right. I will sleep better tonight, knowing he's been arrested. So will Eden."

"Good. See you tomorrow."

Gabriel disconnected the call and set the phone on the nightstand. He turned toward Eden, pulled her into his embrace, and buried his face in her neck.

"They arrested him? Did I hear that right?"

"Yes, Ladybug. It would seem so."

She slumped against him. "So, I'm free to leave the compound now?"

He leaned her back and shook his head. "Your ankle is sprained, and I like it better when I can see you."

"Daddy...I meant when it heals. I'm safe now?"

"You're as safe as anyone else in town, but you're *not* anyone else. You're my Little girl, and you're going to have to deal with the fact that your Daddy is overprotective. Let me absorb this information for five minutes before you start giving me heart palpitations about leaving the compound alone."

She grinned. "Okay, Daddy."

Gabriel carried Eden into the common room the next morning, where everyone was gathered to listen to what King and Doc had to say. The two men looked dog-tired after a three-day shift and a middle-of-the-night call that took most of the night.

Every member of the club who could be there was present. All of them were eager to hear what had happened. They were all piled around the room. Bear and Talon were dragging chairs in from other rooms so everyone could sit.

Gabriel sat in one of the armchairs, keeping Eden on his lap. He carefully propped up her foot even though she insisted it barely hurt anymore. Holding her helped him remain calm when what he really wanted to do was pace the room and get more answers.

Doc began, "As many of you probably heard by now, there was a fire at the Devil's Jesters' compound last night—one of their outbuildings. The fire was started by their recently expelled member, Rat. It turns out this wasn't Rat's first rodeo. He'd previously been arrested for arson two other times."

Everyone gasped.

Gabriel nearly choked. "Why was the man walking the streets free then?"

King took over. "There wasn't enough evidence to convict him the first time, and he served two years the second time. There's very little chance he'll walk free for decades this time. There was significant property damage, and he was caught at the scene."

"Bond?" Gabriel asked.

"Not likely," Doc responded. "Not in a case like this. I'm not a lawyer, of course, but the cops at the scene felt confident."

Gabriel prayed they were right, but he still couldn't stomach the idea of letting Eden out of his sight. He looked around the room to find every other Little girl who had a Daddy in this club, sitting on her Daddy's lap, being held a bit closer than usual this morning, too. They had all felt the effects of living with the constant threat Eden had endured for the past two weeks. Everyone had chipped in to distract her and keep her company. Hell, his brothers had obviously banded together to distract *him*, as well. He'd been a basket case.

Now that Gabriel had the information he needed, he sat quietly, arms wrapped around Eden, and listened while several club members fired off more questions.

Eventually, he tuned them out. Relief flooded him. He set his chin on Eden's shoulder and gently rocked her.

She leaned into him and wrapped her arms around his neck.

When the meeting ended, he carried her back to their suite and straight back to the bedroom. He needed to be with her. He wanted to lie next to her, stare into her eyes, stroke her skin, and thank his lucky stars.

It was ironic that the only reason he'd met her in the first place had been because Rat had harassed her. How ridiculous was it that if Gabriel were to thank anyone for the woman by his side, it would be that asshole, Rat.

Would he have eventually met her through Carlee, anyway? Probably. But instead, he'd met his perfect match on the side of the road where she'd been crying and in need of comfort.

They said nothing for a very long time. Just stared at each other. They were so in tune with each other that his Little girl knew what he needed.

Finally, he inched closer, trying to avoid bonking her foot, and cupped the back of her head so he could kiss her. "I love you," he murmured against her lips.

"I love you, too." She gave him one of her winning smiles. "It's going to be okay, you know."

He nodded.

"I don't have to leave the compound if you don't want me to," she murmured.

He smiled. "Yeah, you do. I'll work up to it. I promise. Just give me some time."

"Okay, Daddy."

"I mean, you can only take so many classes online before you eventually have to attend a few classes on campus."

She frowned. "What are you talking about?"

"College classes, of course. I grabbed the brochure for the local junior college. You can start there. I'm pretty sure you can do a lot of the first year online, but by the second year, you're going to want to—"

Oomph. The air got knocked out of his lungs when his Little girl bolted upright and tackled him so that he fell onto his back next to her. Her eyes were wide and bright. "What are you talking about, Daddy? Stop mincing words."

He chuckled. "I'm talking about you taking classes."

"Are you for real? That costs money. I don't have money."

He lifted a brow. "There is no *I* in *we*, Ladybug. You and I are a unit. Don't you know that yet? We can go to the courthouse and get a license today if you need proof of how much I love and worship you."

"A license," she squealed before swatting him on the chest. "A license for what, you big oaf? A fishing license? Boating? Cause I know you're not talking about a marriage license without even asking me to marry you. That would be very rude. And presumptuous." She pushed out her bottom lip and humphed.

He chuckled as he slid a hand up her back. "I was just trying to get a rise out of you, Ladybug. Mostly because it's so easy and so fun. Of course, I will ask you properly to marry me one day soon. But I want you to stop talking like this is temporary. It's not. It's forever. What's mine is yours and vice versa."

"Daddy, I don't *have* anything."

"Oh, you do. You have a heart of gold. You have love for your old Daddy, who had just about given up on finding a

Little girl to dote on forever and ever. You have sunshine and laughter. You have smiles and giggles. You have a smoking hot body I intend to worship until we're old and gray. So, stop worrying about money. I know you want to go to college, and that's what's going to happen."

She narrowed her gaze at him. "How could you know that? I mentioned it in passing like one time."

He shrugged. "I asked Carlee if you'd ever spoken to her about it, and she told me it had been a dream of yours when you were younger."

She was still staring at him with a skeptical, narrowed gaze. "Did you get hold of the secret notebook and snoop in it, Daddy?"

He lifted both brows. He had not. Now, he kind of wished he had. "No... Why? What does the notebook have to do with anything?"

Her face slowly softened as she stared at him until she finally seemed to believe him. "One day, while we were in one of our blanket forts, we made a list of things we wished we could do."

He pressed his hand flat against her back. "And you listed going to college?"

She nodded.

"I promise I did not look at your secret notebook, Ladybug. I don't even know who has it or where you girls keep it. None of the Daddies would snoop into your private thoughts. That notebook is like a joint diary. It's safe from us, I swear."

"Okay..." She bit into her bottom lip and hesitated. "Do you mean it? For real, I could take some classes?"

"As many as you want."

"As long as they are online..."

He drew in a breath. "I suppose you could take some of them at the campus if you really want to. It wouldn't be until the next semester starts, anyway. I bet I can get over myself enough to at least drive you there and wait outside while you go to class."

He was sort of kidding, but Eden threw herself at him yet again, kissing him all over his face. "Thank you, Daddy. Thank you so much. I promise to be the best student ever, make good grades, and study really hard."

He pulled her down for another kiss. "Be careful with that ankle, Ladybug," he admonished. "And give your Daddy a proper kiss."

She rose to straddle him and then leaned forward and kissed him.

Gabriel pinned her down with his hands on her back, deepening the kiss. He loved it when she straddled him like this. He loved the feel of her pussy against his cock. He was going to love it even more in a minute when he had all her clothes off.

After grabbing the hem of her shirt, he broke the kiss only long enough to yank it over her head.

She moaned against him, already rocking her sexy pussy over his hard cock. Her breasts swayed above him, making him decide to break the kiss so he could watch.

"Damn, you're sexy, Eden," he told her in a deep voice he barely recognized.

Keeping his cock trapped against her pussy, she stopped rocking and smiled down at him. Slowly, she rose so she was sitting straight. She lifted her arms to pull out the bands at the ends of her braids and unraveled them so that her gorgeous curls were freed.

In a sensual lap dance, she tossed her head a few times to let her hair start flying. Her breasts bounced with every move, but the little imp knew exactly what she was doing.

"Are you trying to seduce your Daddy, naughty girl?" His dick was so fucking hard it was going to revolt.

"Maybe?" She arched her chest forward as she lifted her arms higher and ran her fingers through the loose curls.

Gabriel swallowed. *Fuck me.* He was one very lucky bastard. How had he gotten this fortunate?

Eden had been his for two weeks. It seemed like much longer. He couldn't remember what life had been like before he'd picked her up on the side of the road. He'd worked. He'd advised his brothers. He'd cooked. But he hadn't lived.

Now, he was fully alive, and every day was a blessing. Every day, he woke up next to this amazing woman who was his perfect other half. His Little girl. The love of his life. The center of his world.

Yeah, he'd become a worrywart. He would work on that. He didn't like the idea of anyone bothering her or even the possibility that she might fall and get hurt. But she had fallen, and she was going to be fine. In fact, someone had bothered her, and she'd stood up to them, gotten out of the situation, and called for help.

His Little girl was strong. She could take care of herself, but he really hoped that most of the time, she would let him take care of her because that was what he wanted more than anything in the world. He wanted to cherish her and worship her, guide her and nurture her, love her and hold her hand. Everything. He wanted her to have the world, and he intended to give it to her.

Right now, he was mesmerized by the woman above him. She was nothing like the scared girl he'd brought to his suite the night he'd met her. She'd thought sex was nothing interesting. She'd believed she was unattractive.

Gabriel had told her every single day she was beautiful and sexy and perfect. And now his Little girl was so much more confident that she was actually seducing him by holding her arms up and letting her fucking hot tits sway above him.

Was he drooling? Maybe. He finally slid his hands up to cup her breasts and thumbed her pink nipples.

She moaned, her eyes glazed over, and her cheeks turned

pink. She was still easily embarrassed, which was okay because he found it charming.

Gabriel lowered his hands to her pants. "I need these off," he growled.

She leaned forward so her palms were on his chest. "I'll take mine off if you take yours off," she teased, eyes twinkling.

Gabriel sat up and rolled his Little girl to her back on the bed. "Naked," he demanded as he rose to stand, shedding his clothes while she lifted her hips to shrug out of her leggings, panties, and finally, socks.

"Hands and knees," he instructed as he grabbed a condom and rolled it on.

She hesitated. "Hands and knees?"

"Yep."

"Are you going to spank me?" Her voice was a mix of confusion and hope.

He chuckled. "No, Little girl, not today. I'm going to kneel behind you between your legs, grab your hips, and thrust my cock into your wet pussy."

She gave him a slow grin and then scrambled to get into position. "I think I like this plan."

"I know you will, Ladybug."

After he climbed between her legs, he slid his hands up her body, reaching beneath to weigh and fondle her breasts where they swayed under her.

She tipped her head back and moaned. "Daddy…"

He flicked her nipples over and over until she arched her head farther back, panting. "Please…" She thrust her hips back against his cock so that it nestled in between her gorgeous cheeks.

Gabriel eased one hand from her breast to her pussy so he could stroke his fingers through her folds. She was soaked, dripping, and so hot. Her lips were swollen. A few days ago, she had surprised him by shaving her curls off.

That night, he'd sucked her little clit until she'd come three times against his mouth. His naughty girl had writhed and whimpered the entire time. He honestly didn't care if she kept her pussy bare or let the hair grow back. That was up to her. But if it made her feel good to have a smooth pussy, he certainly wasn't going to argue. He loved dragging his beard over her swollen flesh.

"Daddy..." she murmured, squirming against his cock. "I need you."

He eased two fingers into her tight channel and ground his palm into her clit. "Come for Daddy first, and then I'll take this hot pussy with my cock."

She shuddered. His dirty words always made her tremble. He would never get tired of watching her cheeks pinken when he talked dirty to her.

"Come, Eden," he demanded as he thrust his fingers deeper and rubbed her clit harder.

She cried out as her orgasm took over.

Her pussy gripped his fingers so tightly he had to grit his teeth to keep from swapping his fingers for his cock too early. He wanted her to ride this wave first, and then he'd take her there again.

When her orgasm finally subsided, he shifted his hands to her hips and thrust into her.

Eden's groan filled the room. "Ohhhh..."

He eased almost all the way out and then thrust deeper, angling her hips so she would feel his cock against the front of her channel where she got the most pleasure.

He rode her hard because it felt so damn good, and she was obviously enjoying it, too. It was impossible to keep from coming deep inside her earlier than he would have liked. In only a few minutes, he had to give up the battle and let his release pulse out of him.

Eden tipped her pelvis to a new angle and came around his cock a second after him.

Damn, she was precious.

They were both panting as he wrapped an arm around her torso and lowered them onto their sides on the bed without sliding out of her. He spooned her and kissed her neck while he languidly stroked her swollen clit.

"Daddy... That was so good. I love that position."

"I thought you would, Ladybug."

"It made me feel extremely submissive, like we were wolves or something."

He chuckled. "Doggy-style, Little one."

"Yeah. Okay. That. It's nice."

"It's fucking hot is what it is," he told her, chuckling. "I'm glad you liked it. We'll do it again."

"When?" his anxious Little girl asked, eagerness filling her voice.

Both of their bodies shook with his laughter. "Let your old Daddy recover first."

EPILOGUE

T *wo months later…*

"How was class?" Gabriel asked as his Little girl skipped toward him after her first official on-campus class. His heart had been pumping hard the entire time she'd been in the math building, but he'd forced himself to wait outside on a bench in the grassy commons.

Gabriel had worked hard to let go of the reins a bit regarding his Little girl. He had to keep a balance between smothering her to death and keeping her safe. That balance also included the fact that, deep down, he knew she liked his overbearing ways. His insistence on protecting her made her feel loved.

"It was so, so, so, so much fun."

He chuckled as he took her backpack from her and swung it over his shoulder. "Algebra? I've never heard anyone so excited about algebra."

She giggled. "Well, I love going to school. The teacher is

super nice. The kids are pretty nice, too. Most of them are about eight years younger than me, but there was one girl who was close to my age. We sat together. Her name is Adelaine. She was fun. We're going to get together sometime to study."

Gabriel took her hand as he led her to the parking lot. He tried not to react to her announcement. *Get together to study with a classmate?*

Holding his tongue when they reached the SUV, he opened her door and helped her into her seat before setting her backpack on the floorboard.

She started giggling harder and grabbed his bicep after he buckled her seatbelt. "You should see the look on your face. It's so contorted. Does it hurt?"

He narrowed his gaze at her. "Naughty girl."

"Don't worry. I told Adelaine I have the most overprotective boyfriend in the world, and he would probably come along if we met somewhere to study."

"You did, did you?" He couldn't keep from almost grinning. *Score.* "And what did she say to that?"

"She swooned and asked if you have any brothers."

Gabriel lifted both brows. "I have a lot of brothers. Is she Little?"

Eden rolled her eyes. "I don't know that yet, Daddy. I certainly didn't lead with that question."

"Of course not. Silly me," he joked. Still leaning through her door, he kissed her. "I don't think you should have told her I'm your boyfriend, though. It gives the wrong impression."

Eden frowned. "Why not? Aren't you my boyfriend?"

He shook his head as he reached into his pocket and pulled out the small pink velvet box he'd been carrying around for weeks while waiting for the perfect opportunity to give it to her.

She gasped when he held it in front of her. "What is that?"

"It's a symbol that moves me out of the boyfriend zone and into the fiancé zone. You want to see it?" he teased.

She giggled again. "Daddy, that is not a proposal."

He chuckled. He'd known she would react that way if he presented her with a ring and such a ridiculous pronouncement. "How about if you just hold this little box while I drive us home." He opened her hand, set the pink box on her palm, and curled her fingers around it.

Leaving her breathless and without words, he shut her door and rounded to his side of the car.

"Seriously?" she asked a few minutes later as he drove away from campus, ignoring the ring he'd asked her to hold without showing it to her.

"Anticipation is good for Little girls," he said, glancing at her with a wink.

"Daddy, that's just mean." She gripped the box against her chest, practically petting the velvet.

Ten minutes later, he pulled into the compound, parked the car, and rounded to help her down from her seat.

Her jaw hung down as he grabbed her backpack. "What should we make for dinner tonight?" he asked.

"Daddy!" She held the box in one hand as he took her other hand to lead her toward the clubhouse.

When he opened the door and ushered her into the large common room in front of him, he grinned behind her. Every one of his brothers and their Littles who could be there were gathered in the large room. They all yelled, "Surprise!"

Eden stopped walking two steps into the room, causing Gabriel to crowd against her to shut the door. "What's all this?" she asked.

"It's an engagement party," Carlee exclaimed, clapping her hands. "Did you like the ring? Did you say yes?"

Eden turned her head to shoot Gabriel a glare.

God, he loved her. He carefully took the small box from her hand, rounded in front of her, and dropped to one knee. "Eden Zimbel, I love you more than life itself. You've made me the happiest man and Daddy alive. Will you do me the honor of being my wife?"

She clapped a hand over her mouth, tears running down her face.

"Is that a yes?" Gabriel teased.

She nodded before lowering her hand and whispering, "Yes."

Gabriel finally opened the box to reveal the solitaire he'd chosen for his future wife. He pulled it out, took her hand, and slid it onto her finger. It fit perfectly because he'd watched which rings she used on which fingers for weeks before discreetly taking one to have it sized at the jewelry store.

Eden held her hand in front of her, fingers spread, staring at the ring without blinking. Finally, she launched herself into Gabriel's arms so hard and fast he nearly toppled over onto his ass.

He wrapped his arms around her and lifted her as he stood before twirling her around in a circle. "Do you like it, Ladybug?"

"I love it, Daddy." She grinned from ear to ear. "It's so pretty. I'll never take it off."

Chanting started in the room with one of the Littles until all of them shouted, "Kiss, kiss, kiss…"

Gabriel cupped the back of Eden's head and brought his lips to hers. "I love you," he whispered against them.

"I love you, too, Daddy."

And then they kissed to the cheers of everyone in the room.

AUTHOR'S NOTE

I hope you're enjoying the Shadowridge Guardians MC series as much as we are enjoying writing them! The next book in the series is Talon by Pepper North.

Shadowridge Guardians MC
Steele by Pepper North
Kade by Kate Oliver
Atlas by Becca Jameson
Doc by Kate Oliver
Gabriel by Becca Jameson
Talon by Pepper North
Bear by Becca Jameson
Faust by Pepper North
Storm by Kate Oliver

Combining the sizzling talents of bestselling authors Pepper North, Kate Oliver, and Becca Jameson, the Shadowridge Guardians are guaranteed to give you a thrill and leave you dreaming of your own throbbing motorcycle joyride.

Are you daring enough to ride with a club of rough, growly,

commanding men? The protective Daddies of the Shadowridge Guardians Motorcycle Club will stop at nothing to ensure the safety and protection of everything that belongs to them: their Littles, their club, and their town. Throw in some sassy, naughty, mischievous women who won't hesitate to serve their fair share of attitude even in the face of looming danger, and this brand new MC Romance series is ready to ignite!

ALSO BY BECCA JAMESON

Seattle Doms:

Salacious Exposure

Salacious Desires By Kate Oliver

Salacious Attraction

Salacious Devotion

Danger Bluff:

Rocco

Hawking

Kestrel

Magnus

Phoenix

Caesar

Roses and Thorns:

Marigold

Oleander

Jasmine

Tulip

Daffodil

Lily

Bite of Pain Anthology: Gemma's Release

Shadowridge Guardians:

Steele by Pepper North

Kade by Kate Oliver

Atlas by Becca Jameson

Doc by Kate Oliver

Gabriel by Becca Jameson

Talon by Pepper North

Bear by Becca Jameson

Faust by Pepper North

Storm by Kate Oliver

Blossom Ridge:

Starting Over

Finding Peace

Building Trust

Feeling Brave

Embracing Joy

Accepting Love

Blossom Ridge Box Set One

Blossom Ridge Box Set Two

The Wanderers:

Sanctuary

Refuge

Harbor

Shelter

Hideout

Haven

The Wanderers Box Set One

The Wanderers Box Set Two

Surrender:

Raising Lucy

Teaching Abby

Leaving Roman

Choosing Kellen

Pleasing Josie

Honoring Hudson

Nurturing Britney

Charming Colton

Convincing Leah

Rewarding Avery

Impressing Brett

Guiding Cassandra

Surrender Box Set One

Surrender Box Set Two

Surrender Box Set Three

Open Skies:

Layover

Redeye

Nonstop

Standby

Takeoff

Jetway

Open Skies Box Set One

Open Skies Box Set Two

Shadow SEALs:

Shadow in the Desert

Shadow in the Darkness

Holt Agency:

Rescued by Becca Jameson

Unchained by KaLyn Cooper

Protected by Becca Jameson

Liberated by KaLyn Cooper

Defended by Becca Jameson

Unrestrained by KaLyn Cooper

Delta Team Three (Special Forces: Operation Alpha):

Destiny's Delta

Canyon Springs:

Caleb's Mate

Hunter's Mate

Corked and Tapped:

Volume One: Friday Night

Volume Two: Company Party

Volume Three: The Holidays

Project DEEP:

Reviving Emily

Reviving Trish

Reviving Dade

Reviving Zeke

Reviving Graham

Reviving Bianca

Reviving Olivia

Project DEEP Box Set One

Project DEEP Box Set Two

SEALs in Paradise:

Hot SEAL, Red Wine

Hot SEAL, Australian Nights

Hot SEAL, Cold Feet

Hot SEAL, April's Fool

Hot SEAL, Brown-Eyed Girl

Dark Falls:

Dark Nightmares

Club Zodiac:

Training Sasha

Obeying Rowen

Collaring Brooke

Mastering Rayne

Trusting Aaron

Claiming London

Sharing Charlotte

Taming Rex

Tempting Elizabeth

Club Zodiac Box Set One

Club Zodiac Box Set Two

Club Zodiac Box Set Three

The Art of Kink:

Pose

Paint

Sculpt

Arcadian Bears:

Grizzly Mountain

Grizzly Beginning

Grizzly Secret

Grizzly Promise

Grizzly Survival

Grizzly Perfection

Arcadian Bears Box Set One

Arcadian Bears Box Set Two

Sleeper SEALs:

Saving Zola

Spring Training:

Catching Zia

Catching Lily

Catching Ava

Spring Training Box Set

The Underground series:

Force

Clinch

Guard

Submit

Thrust

Torque

The Underground Box Set One

The Underground Box Set Two

Wolf Masters series:

Kara's Wolves

Lindsey's Wolves

Jessica's Wolves

Alyssa's Wolves

Tessa's Wolf

Rebecca's Wolves

Melinda's Wolves

Laurie's Wolves

Amanda's Wolves

Sharon's Wolves

Wolf Masters Box Set One

Wolf Masters Box Set Two

Claiming Her series:

The Rules

The Game

The Prize

Claiming Her Box Set

Emergence series:

Bound to be Taken

Bound to be Tamed

Bound to be Tested

Bound to be Tempted

Emergence Box Set

The Fight Club series:

Come

Perv

Need

Hers

Want

Lust

The Fight Club Box Set One

The Fight Club Box Set Two

Wolf Gatherings series:

Tarnished

Dominated

Completed

Redeemed

Abandoned

Betrayed

Wolf Gatherings Box Set One

Wolf Gathering Box Set Two

Durham Wolves series:

Rescue in the Smokies

Fire in the Smokies

Freedom in the Smokies

Durham Wolves Box Set

Stand Alone Books:

Blind with Love

Guarding the Truth

Out of the Smoke

Abducting His Mate

Wolf Trinity

Frostbitten

A Princess for Cale / A Princess for Cain

Severed Dreams

Where Alphas Dominate

ABOUT THE AUTHOR

Becca Jameson is a USA Today best-selling author of over 140 books. She is well-known for her Wolf Masters series, her Fight Club series, and her Surrender series. She currently lives in Houston, Texas, with her husband. Two grown kids pop in every once in a while too! She is loving this journey and has dabbled in a variety of genres, including paranormal, sports romance, military, reverse harem, dark romance, suspense, dystopian, and BDSM.

A total night owl, Becca writes late at night, sequestering herself in her office with a glass of red wine and a bar of dark chocolate, her fingers flying across the keyboard as her characters weave their own stories.

During the day--which never starts before ten in the morning!--she can be found walking, running errands, or reading in her favorite hammock chair!

...where Alphas dominate...

Becca's Newsletter Sign-up

Join my Facebook fan group, Becca's Bibliomaniacs, for the most up-to-date information, random excerpts while I work, giveaways, and fun release parties!

Facebook Fan Group:
Becca's Bibliomaniacs

Contact Becca:
www.beccajameson.com
beccajameson4@aol.com

f facebook.com / becca.jameson.18
X x.com / beccajameson
⊙ instagram.com / becca.jameson
BB bookbub.com / authors / becca-jameson
g goodreads.com / beccajameson
a amazon.com / author / beccajameson

Printed in Great Britain
by Amazon

37946087R00116